blueprint

Brigitte,

I hope you enjoy this comical
side of life, and life after
death.

Lynnette Vaughn

LYNNETTE VAUGHN

RUBY
READ

Blueprint
First published in Australia in 2006
by Ruby Read Publishing

Copyright © 2006, Lynnette Vaughn

Project management: Best Legenz
www.bestlegenz.com.au

The National Library of Australia
Cataloguing-in-Publication entry

Vaughn, Lynnette, 1964- .
Blueprint.
ISBN 0 9775535 0 7.

I. Title.

A823.4

Editor: Monica Dennison
Cover design: Kylie Prats
Internal design: Best Legenz
Printed in Australia by Griffin Press
www.LynnetteVaughn.com

Acknowledgements

To my real life 'Guardian Angels'—my Mother Doreen, Father Albert, and Step Mother Linda, who guide me from across the globe. Thank you for your support and especially your love.

Thank you to my sister Cynthia…who is not only a living Angel, but my best friend. Your love and support is a gift which I will treasure forever!

To the 'dinner party' characters and my real life beloved friends…Mary and David, Sophia, Jason, Mike, Jimmi, Carole, Sasha, Grace, and Ben you have impacted my life in Australia more than you think… thank you for your friendship!

Helen Elward…thank you for working so hard on this book and managing everything! You are an amazing woman. Also to Kylie, Monica, Jodie and Bernice —I thank you for everything, you helped make this happen!

Elena, you always saw me as a writer—well here is the proof! Thank you for your support!

As well many of my friends who I don't see often, but I never stop thinking of…Anne, Shelley, Lindsay, Marcia, Deanna, Scot, Ammy, Darienne, Monika, and Drew.

Hazel, you helped me understand my own Blueprint, thank you!

There are specific people who impacted me, but are no longer in my life…I thank you for the lessons I had to learn from you. Hopefully, when we meet up in Heaven, we'll have our own dinner party with lots of wine and laugh about everything that happened!

This book is dedicated to those who have influenced my life, but who are now watching from Heaven...
Grandmothers—Anna and Christine,
Grandfathers—Jacob and Emil,
and friend Suzanne.

Prologue
Heaven, a Narrative

*H*ello I'm Oran, one of four Angels that work in the First Triad choir. Would you believe I report directly to God? My performance reviews are a little daunting, to say the least, but I've been in my position for thousands of years, so I must be doing something right.

Since I've got a lot of time on my hands, I keep myself busy meeting with colleagues, attending lectures and debating why humans are so confused about what happens after they die. We here find it frustrating that so many humans are agnostic and believe that death is final. Perhaps you are thinking, "What's Heaven's like?" Well…You've probably heard the stories about near death experiences…and the white light. Well, it's true! There's a lot of white here as it's a popular color. Let's see, what else? Well, we have no requirement to sleep, eat or drink…as our bodies are more organic than on Earth.

What does it look like? There's a constant temperature of around 26°C, beautiful lush gardens and colors beyond a human's optical range—don't forget we are in a different dimension. Likewise, sounds are much richer— higher octaves and deeper basses than you've heard before. Everything in Heaven is serene, tranquil and exquisite.

When you first arrive, Heaven looks exactly as you want it to. Why? Well the best example I could give you is from Richard Matheson's book (that later became a movie) What Dreams May Come. *In the film version, Robin Williams, who is the lead male, dies in an automobile accident…when he crosses over, he finds his new Heavenly surroundings remind him of the paintings created by his wife. As he becomes comfortable with his surroundings, the real Heaven appears—complete with homes, lecture halls, theatres, libraries and many buildings.*

We have a higher vibrational frequency than humans. Though some mediums can see, hear or feel us, to the average individual, we remain hidden. You might have heard there are eleven dimensions, well that's correct— and a few more if you are lucky to work close to God.

At this time, I am observing two souls who are sitting next to a stream that joins a larger lake at the bottom. Although they have had hundreds of reincarnations—and hundreds of names, in Heaven they are known as Arielle and Raphael. They look different from what they did on Earth, but why wouldn't they? They have each lived many lives both as man and woman. Arielle always says, "A body is like a piece of clothing, you wear it when you are born, and then discard it when you die."

This evening Raphael is hosting a special dinner party for Arielle. The theme of this party is a surprise—however Raphael has requested all guests dress in white. Why white you ask? Well white contains all the colors in a rainbow and has the highest vibration energy possible. I guess he wants to ensure the evening is energy-packed.

This story is about Arielle's journey in planning her last Blueprint and incarnation and what happens when friends take over.

1

Raphael and Arielle

Raphael is sitting on a deck chair reading a book. Although his soul is thousands of years old, his physical appearance is that of a man in his mid 40s— salt and pepper hair, a grey beard and his skin, which is showing signs of aging, has an olive complexion.

Arielle is Raphael's soul mate. They have been together for thousands of years, that is unless one feels a desire to try a new life, or is specifically asked by the Council to. When this happens, they prepare their Blueprint – its' theme, who they'll be, how they'll participate in each other's life and ask if any friends wish to partake. They have always gone together.

At this moment, Arielle is standing painting a landscape scene of the lake which is below her. Her long, natural, red hair accentuates her porcelain, skin. Not bad for a woman thousands of years old. Who said skin care wouldn't be of any use?

Raphael places his book on the table, turns to Arielle, and says, "I have been thinking."

She raises her eyebrows. "Oh?"

"I know you're last incarnation is coming up—soon you'll be leaving." Arielle smiles in interest (and continues to listen). "I was wondering…could I help plan it? Your last life was so traumatic, and…I don't want a repeat of what actions you took."

Arielle frowns at her partner. "I know—my suicide attempt was stupid. I thought it was my only way out of a terrible situation." She reaches over to hold his hand. "Thank goodness it failed. Did I ever thank you for coming to my rescue? You turned everything around for me my darling." Arielle places her paint brush down on the table and turns to directly face Raphael. "This incarnation is too important and I've been told by the Council that I must do it perfectly, no exceptions. I need to ensure my Blueprint details are well planned—including personality traits, lessons, who will be my parents, siblings, friends and children, where I'll live, my occupation and my overall theme. Raphael, are you sure you won't change your mind about returning with me?"

Raphael shakes his head. "No, I'm sorry my love."

She pleads, "But you are my soul mate, how will I ever endure this next life without you?"

"You know that we can have many soul mates throughout our existence, but I have concluded my lessons and incarnations, I am only waiting for you to complete yours. Besides, the Council won't let me!"

"Hmm, good point...but hopefully if all goes well, I'll have my new promotion."

"That's what I'm counting on. You have lots of friends ready to spring to your assistance, including myself. Who's your Spirit Guide this time?"

"I assume it'll be Cynthia again. She's been with me nearly all of my incarnations—I have an appointment with the Council next week, so I'll find out then."

"I met with the Council last week?" says Raphael.

"Oh? Why?"

"They encouraged me to organize a brainstorming session with your friends...so tonight at our dinner party, I thought of an amusing group activity."

Arielle raises her eyebrows with a worried look.

Raphael laughs. "Don't worry! It'll be fun. I thought we'd have everyone suggest certain scenarios—then we'll dissect them to ensure every detail is thought of..."

Arielle is delighted, however before she is allowed to respond, Raphael continues, "I've already thought of a few twists for you."

Arielle laughs. "I'm sure you have, I know you'll try to get me back for causing your last midlife crisis.

Perhaps we'd better get back so we can get things organized."

They both stand and with a sweep of their hands, their table, chairs, easel, paints and books all disappear. They look at each other, smile, then instantly vanish.

2
The Dinner Guests

The dining room is entirely white. In the corner of the room is an enormous white plastered fireplace with a roaring fire burning inside. In the centre of the room stands a large white dining table with fifteen white leather chairs surrounding it. On top of the white linen tablecloth sits antique white china, elegant silverware and delicate crystal. In front of each place setting, is a name card written in calligraphy. Two large candelabras sit on each end of the table—each with eight white candles. There are various candles scattered throughout the room.

Raphael enters the room and places two bottles of wine on the table. One of label reads 'Mount Gisborne Pinot Noir' and the second "Mount Gisborne, Chardonnay," He whispers to himself, "It's been a while since I've enjoyed a great drop!"

Arielle walks in the room just as he turns around and asks, "What are you mumbling about?" She looks at the wine bottles and comments, "Ooh... great choice my love!"

Moments later the doorbell rings out with the sound of angels singing. It plays for several seconds which is enough time for her to walk to the door. She peers through the peep-hole then laughs when she sees a distorted close up of the group huddled together smiling back at her. She opens the door and says, "Hello!"

Thirteen guests walk in carrying baskets of fruit, vegetables, wine and flowers. They too are all wearing white and, as they walk past Arielle, they lean and kiss her cheek.

They walk into the dining room, and are excited to see the elaborately decorated table and room filled with burning candles. They place their items down, find their name card, then take their seat...waiting for the festivities to commence.

The guests include:

Sophia—All of her past lives have been involved in religion. Her reincarnation themes and desires were to understand spirituality by experiencing every organized religion known to humankind. Sophia is attractive, five foot eight in height, long dark brown hair and of Mediterranean decent. Her vibrant personality can inspire anyone.

Scott—He has eccentric ideas and likes to shock people. He is five foot nine, of English decent and has sandy brown short hair. His friendly personality is made even more noticeable when he smiles, as his adorable dimples light up the room.

Carole—Her last life on Earth was very traumatic, so she is very apprehensive about going back and trying again. She is five foot six with strawberry blonde hair and pale clear skin. She is fun. She dresses with a sense of style and sophistication and always tells a good joke.

David—His reincarnations have all been to experience the same lesson over and over…that of patience. He has wisdom and maturity. David is in his 50s, with brown-grey hair, about five foot eight, medium build and wears glasses.

Michael—Is a handsome European gentleman, and very popular with the ladies. Though he has had several incarnations to other planets, he has never been to Earth. He is five foot nine, has dark olive skin, dark brown hair and eyes. His personality is kind and gentle, and is very entertaining.

Elena—Is the resident occult expert. She is tall, and has a feisty personality. She provides Arielle with answers to many of her questions regarding astrology, numerology and writing a Blueprint. Elena tries to educate everyone at the dinner party on why souls take great care and detail planning their next life.

Mary—Is an old soul. All of her lessons were to develop trust and confidence. She is composed, sympathetic and thoughtful. Most of her incarnations have been in teaching professions. Mary is of medium height, has short brown curly hair, and wears round glasses.

Jimmy—Is a counselor in Heaven. He is a free spirit and full of creativity He has the ability to bring out everyone's true desires by offering encouragement, and support. He encourages Arielle to push herself into new experiences. He is five foot seven, has a handsome face and warm brown eyes.

Linda—Is the cheerleader of the group and is full of energy. She encourages everyone to give everything a go. She is five foot eight, has silver grey hair, a contagious laugh, and beautiful flawless porcelain skin.

Jason—Is shy, demure and sophisticated. He enjoys nature and the tranquility of the countryside. Most of his past lives have involved medicine in some form. Jason is five foot nine, handsome with brown hair and eyes.

Saskia—Her reincarnations have all been located in Europe—Russia, Scandinavia, Germany and Czechoslovakia. She is bubbly, fun to be around, energetic and very interesting. She is fit and healthy—with petite features, long blonde hair, sparkling green eyes and a flawless radiant complexion.

Grace—Is an Indonesian beauty. Her name reflects her personality – refined. Her appeal is her individuality and ability to make people feel good about themselves. She is tall, elegant and always has a smile on her face. She's only had two incarnations to Earth—however, they were two hundred years ago.

Benjamin—Is a boisterous long-haired Aussie surfer, yet is a perfect gentleman. His energy is captivating as is his laugh. Benjamin is in his late twenties and loves to talk.

3
The Dinner Party

Arielle walks into the dining room from the kitchen, sets a large cheese tray on the table and then moves to the opposite end to take her seat. As she sits, she notices her wine glass is empty so she quickly jumps up, picks up the bottle of Pinot Noir, fills her glass, then sits back down.

Raphael stands at the table and taps his wine glass with his small desert spoon to gain everyone's attention. "Thank you all for coming this evening. We have something rather exciting to share with you tonight…in a very short while, Arielle will undertake one last incarnation to Earth and to celebrate this occasion, we have planned an amusing night for you all…Arielle would like your help planning her final Blueprint."

Suddenly there is silence.

Everyone looks around at one another. Linda asks, "But Raphael, it's not customary for friends to work on someone else's Blueprint."

"Isn't the responsibility Arielle's, along with her Spirit Guide and the Council?" asks Mary.

Raphael takes his seat. "True, but there's a reason why we need your input tonight. Arielle has been reincarnated a total of 249 times and her next return will be her final journey to Earth. The Council have requested that Arielle plan and execute her Blueprint exactly as prepared, with no exceptions and if she does this, she will receive a substantial promotion."

"What do you need us to do?" asks Linda.

"I was just about to get to that. Arielle needs our help with brainstorming ideas…I thought one by one we could suggest potential scenarios…then analyse whether it would be substantial enough to gain the Council's approval. Are you game?"

Everyone smiles and nods simultaneously.

Raphael continues, "Great, so let the games begin! First we need to decide Arielle's sex—will she be a he or she? Second, geographic's—where and when she'll be born. Then we'll need to propose suggestions for personality characteristics, will he or she be poor or wealthy, etcetera."

Raphael looks directly at Elena. "Would you mind helping with birth dates? You used to study the occult, specifically numerology, right?"

Elena says, "Yes, and tarot cards…oh and astrology."

Raphael moves to the edge of his chair placing his elbows on the table. "Excluding Michael, most of us here have all experienced living on Earth at least once. Grace, it's been over two hundred years since you've returned, so for Michael and your benefit, I'll review the processes of creating a Blueprint."

Michael asks, "Do we go through the same process for going to Earth as we do for other planets?

"No. Earth is the only planet of free will and choice—each soul decides their mission for their life and this journey becomes their destiny. As for other planets, the Council just tell us what they want us to do there."

Grace asks, "Does everyone accomplish their Blueprints?"

Raphael answers, "Some do…some don't, and some…well they start with good intentions but go way off track for some reason."

"Why can't we remember what our Blueprint is when we are on Earth?" asks Michael.

"Well, in Heaven we can remember everything…all of our Blueprints, past lives, persons whom we have shared lives with, places we have visited, lived, and so on. However when Arielle returns, she'll not have access to this information, it is in her subconscious and can be accessed only by dreams or psychics."

Mary asks, "What kind of promotion are they offering you Arielle?"

"They have offered me an Archangel position—in fact, working along side Archangel Gabriel."

The guests all gasp with excitement, then clap.

Sophia not only claps but yells out. "Oh, well done Arielle! You must have really impressed God!"

"I don't know about that...and I still have to succeed first!"

Raphael smiles. "That's where you all come in. To ensure she's ready, I have arranged with the Council for our dinner party group to act as her pre-birth Council."

Everyone starts to speak at once with excitement. Raphael has to raise his hand to bring control over the group.

Michael asks, "Pre-birth council? What's that?"

Raphael answers, "Well, it's simply a specialized group who help counsel a soul prior to their incarnation. They discuss why they want to return, a tentative agenda, etc...it would have been similar to what you discussed with the Council for your journey to Mars."

David waves his hand.

"Yes David?"

"Why is there so much controversy about reincarnation? If so many have returned at one point or another, why do so many on Earth not believe?"

Raphael replies, "Good question David. Humans are all born with the knowledge, in fact some children can recall past life experiences or even recognize persons from a previous life."

Grace asks, "Is that why some babies make strange or instantly warm to someone?"

Arielle adds, "Perhaps."

"Some young children have 'imaginary friends' who might be a deceased relative who hasn't yet gone to the light, or their Spirit Guide—who appears as a child playmate and gives them advice. If parents actually listened to their children when they are playing with these 'friends,' they'd hear some interesting things," says Raphael.

Mary laughs, "Kids do say the strangest things… one day out of the blue, my daughter justified her reason for coming to Earth—then proceeded to sing a song in French."

"What's wrong with that?" asks Linda

"We lived in South Africa, we didn't speak French, nor ever taught her."

"Oh, that is strange then."

David asks, "If some children can remember past lives…why not adults?"

"You are just full of questions tonight, aren't you?" laughs Elena.

Raphael chuckles. "Some children seem to remember people, places and like your daughter

Linda, languages they might have spoken in a past life. Children also have no fear when talking to spirits, Angels or Spirit Guides about their past...but they seem to loose this ability somewhere between the age of six and eight years old...just as they are entering school."

Arielle says, "Actually, there's a more significant reason why adults don't remember past lives...they're not supposed to."

Raphael clarifies, "Just imagine the chaos if they did?"

David then says, "Hmm, egos...I understand! If they returned knowing who their past enemies or previous lovers were, they might waste their life hunting them down instead of living out their purpose. But if you can go to any planet, why do you want to go back to Earth Arielle?"

"Earth is paradise! And it's the only planet with gravity and where souls can learn to balance the physical world with a spiritual one. Earth is the only planet with the freedom to be anyone I want...and well...I want to experience it one last time."

"And don't forget, God asked you to!" says Sophia.

Grace asks, "But why would God care where a soul goes, or what destiny a soul has on Earth? What's in it for God?"

Raphael says, "Interesting question Grace! All souls are part of a higher spiritual force...some call it 'God Force,' and many religions call God different names, but everything in the Universe is part of a higher power."

Arielle looks at Sophia. "Sophia will no doubt explain Earth religion later, but for Heaven to fully evolve, God needs to comprehend each and every Blueprint scenario, every soul's life theme and understand why a soul has a desire, then what it feels like to fulfill that desire, or fail."

David laughs. "Like work experience?"

"Well yes David—that's it exactly! We all leave with the best of intentions...but when we get to Earth, we get caught up with families, jobs, pleasures, and money!"

Michael asks, "So then, a Blueprint describes a theme and outlines our life on Earth. It includes who'll be part of our lives...some lovers, enemies, friends, in one life, then mothers, fathers or children in the next. As well, what we intend to do when we get there."

Raphael nods. "Perfect."

"Arielle, do you remember our last life together? I was your husband Robert—boy was I a jerk! He, or rather I, beat you...Arielle, I'm so sorry!" says Mary.

Scott jumps in, "Yes, and I was your son...you always looked out for me."

Raphael frowns in frustration and says, "Come on guys, we're in Heaven now...no one holds any judgment or remorse toward one another."

Elena adds, "That's right Raphael, and if we analyzed everything now, you'd understand why she selected Mary as her husband Robert, and Scott as her son. Certain behaviours were required for not only Arielle to learn and grow, but Scott and Mary."

"Well put!" states Raphael.

Mary continues, "During my life as Robert, my life theme was to be an intimidator—so everyone saw me as manipulating, dominating and angry. When I returned to Heaven, I was told that my actions were required to push Arielle and those around her into certain behaviours. However, instead of standing up to me, Arielle withdrew, she became very insecure and blamed herself for causing Scott to run away."

"Yes and I tried to kill myself."

"But you didn't...did you? Instead Sophia and I helped you. I accidently pushed you into Sophia, who was incarnated as Father Tim. When he knocked you down, he saw your tears...then he sat and listened to your problems. Once you gained your confidence, you stood up for yourself and walked away from Robert. Your theme of victim was conquered when you finally got the courage to leave him," Raphael adds.

Scott suddenly looks at David and says, "I've just remembered the day I died. I was shot in a rice field somewhere in Vietnam and I can still remember the experience of crossing over, it was so strange. I could hear people talking, yet I couldn't move. I felt lightheaded like I was floating. Then I saw a white light which gave the most overwhelming feeling of love. I looked down…I could see myself lying on the grass, but I kept thinking what was I doing floating when my body was on the ground? Then I arrived in a reception type room and when I looked around there were people who had passed away with me, or before me. I was convinced I was dreaming, but I wasn't! Many spirits came to help me, by just holding my hand or standing beside me. Others talked to me and helped me realize that I was really dead."

Scott pauses then asks, "Arielle, there is one thing that has always puzzled me, why do some souls choose to go back after living such traumatic lives?"

"May I answer this Arielle?"

"Go ahead Raphiel."

"After time in Heaven you forget everything—your ego, any pain or joy you experienced on Earth. Then one day you decide to give it another go."

Sophia laughs. "Some look at living on Earth as a game…they keep going back over and over until they get it right."

Arielle adds, "The ones who do get it right, followed their gut feeling, or perhaps paid attention to their dreams. Of course there are others who made a mess of it."

David asks, "How do they get back on track? Do they have a midlife crisis then?"

"That's a good question," says Arielle. "Some do. They quit their jobs, leave their partners, travel across the world or go back to university to study something completely different."

Linda interrupts, "Raphael, I heard that when a human reaches their mid-thirties the friends or loved ones around them are actually souls who have subconsciously found them for a reason. Is this correct?"

"I guess it seems probable—in fact, imagine if your Blueprint destiny was to be a teacher...but instead you were an accountant. Everyday you went to work...hating your life, wanting to change your job, but you didn't know what to do and nor did you have the courage."

Carole adds, "Perhaps you prayed for help."

Grace smiles. "Oh, I get it...this is where fate steps in...right?"

Raphael continues, "Yes, and one evening you meet someone who puts an idea into your head... something like, you should be a mathematics teacher. From that day forward it's all you can think about. You already know the maths side, so you go back to university for your teaching certificate and change your destiny."

"So very true Raphael," says Arielle. "All a human need do is ask for help...then God, Angels, Spirit Guides and workers are sent to the rescue."

Raphael adds, "But there is a sense of order—everything must happen in its correct time...even death. Sometimes you need to experience being loved, to give love...or be rejected, to understand what the other person is feeling when you reject them."

Michael suddenly says, "I feel sad for humans who are so afraid of dying."

Arielle says, "Well, so do I Michael. Their physical life on Earth is only a small portion of their soul's life. They shouldn't grieve for the dead, but understand the soul has moved on to something else."

Linda smiles. "Many lifetimes ago, I was told an old Hindu fable which I think is very appropriate now. Would you mind if I told you?"

Everyone nods in agreement.

Linda stands and addresses her friends. "The fable is about a caterpillar who is nearing the end of his crawling phase...he informs his friends that he will be leaving them soon. He becomes depressed and overcome with sadness, farewells his friends and says, 'Tomorrow I shall be no more.' The next day this caterpillar stops breathing and his friends assume he has died. They are tormented with sadness as they know a similar fate is coming to them as well. The friends give up. They stop living and say, 'What for, we are only going to die anyways.' The irony of this little fable is the ignorance of the caterpillar and all caterpillars thereafter. He did not die, rather he transformed into a chrysalis-larva and soon emerged into a beautiful butterfly. His new physical form was now capable of new and exciting adventures. And this too is the same fate for all humans on Earth."

There is silence. No one moves. Then at once they break out into applause and cheers.

Raphael stands. "That's fantastic Linda, I haven't heard of this fable, but that explains everyone's fate of life and death perfectly. Bravo!"

Arielle joins in, "Families and friends, like that of the caterpillars, can become so caught up the grief of death that their souls remain 'stuck' on Earth. Some spirits hang around not knowing what to do as they haven't realized that they are dead."

Mary asks, "Is that what is meant by an Earth-bound soul?"

"Yes as an Earth-bound soul is someone who chooses not to go to the light, or doesn't know it's there."

Mary asks again, "What do they do then?"

"Well, if humans experience a sudden traumatic death—a painful illness, violence, or an act of God, they may be in shock. It can take centuries to accept they have died, so they just hang around Earth, living their old lives."

Jason, who has been quite most of the evening says, "That's so sad. Isn't there anyone who can help them?"

Arielle smiles. "Of course. There are special people on Earth who are able to help spirits cross over."

"Oh, like those television shows on Earth about mediums or that lady who help spirits cross over."

"Yes Jason, just like them. When they finally do cross over, there are counselors in Heaven, just like on Earth."

Jimmy reaches over for the wine bottle and empties the contents into his glass. "If you don't mind, I'd like to volunteer as someone in your next life. Would you write me into your Blueprint? Are there any parts for me?"

"Don't worry Arielle, if Jimmy gets you into trouble and you go off track, we'll send in a rescue squad," says Sophia.

"I believe you're all enjoying this? Why not make it into a soap-opera then?"

"Great idea, let's call it *The Days of your Soul's Journey*," Jimmy adds, making everyone laugh.

"Ha ha! Why not put my life on HeavTel's comedy channel too," says Arielle sarcastically as she stands and walks over to the wine rack to select another bottle for her guests.

Linda sees Arielle coming back with a new bottle of wine, she drinks the contents of her glass and holds it out to be refilled then exclaims, "Great Idea! I know an executive producer, I'll call him tomorrow; it will be a smash hit."

Arielle says laughing, "But…I was only joking!"

Raphael leaves the room while everyone is talking and laughing about the possibilities of this soap opera. He returns pushing in a white board on wheels. He maneuvers it so everyone can view the board. "Okay you guys, enough serious talk, it's time for fun! I'll leave you to clear the table…while I get something…"

Linda stands and proclaims, "I love Heaven—no need for dishwashers!"

She starts by sweeping her arm over the table—food, cutlery, candles and plates begin to disappear. Others join in by sweeping their arms over their section of the table but just as someone was about to sweep the wine bottle away, Raphael returns and quickly reaches across the table to save it. "Not the wine, not the wine! We need this for inspiration." He pours himself another glass of wine and then starts writing on the whiteboard. "Okay, Arielle you may wish to explain the process so everyone knows what is expected."

4 The Blueprint Desire

Arielle stands and walks to the whiteboard. "You're right Raphael, there is a lot of background that needs to be prepared, and we just can't start creating scenarios out of the blue. I'll need to give you all some boundaries. Let me explain." She writes on the whiteboard.

1. Desire
2. Planning
3. Timing

"Well then, the first number is Desire…" she turns around and faces the group, "my desire is the most important reason for my return—besides a substantial promotion if I manage to pull it off!"

She sees Scott sitting quietly in his chair, his jaw resting on his palm and staring into space deep in thought. "Scott, where are you? What are you thinking so hard about?"

Scott smiles. "Oh sorry, Arielle. I was paying attention, only I was wondering…you mentioned your desire, but what about lessons? Do you already know what they'll be?"

"Well, yes and no…Elena will discuss numerology later, as it will cover lessons I can give myself, however when the Council review the Akashic records and my past lives, they will notify me of any specific lesson they want me to experience."

Scott butts in, "I don't understand Akashic Records. What are they and why are they reviewed?"

Arielle tries to explain, "Do you remember after you died and returned to Heaven?

"Yes."

"And after a period of rest you were taken to a large library full of records?"

Scott thinks. "Yes I do! I remember this massive hall that was filled with millions of leather bound books."

"What else do you remember?"

"This very old man told me there is a file on every reincarnated life I have ever lived, not only for my life, but for every soul in the universe. He showed me my last life, but rather than the words appearing in a book, my life appeared in hieroglyphics. I saw every detail, felt every emotion and learned what I had accomplished, or hadn't. He also showed me what my last lesson was."

Carole asks, "Out of interest, what was it Scott?"

Scott chuckles. "It was to be humble...I guess I didn't quite master that one! Instead, I was the opposite—egotistical, arrogant and self-centered. In my next life, he said, I will have to reattempt this lesson or it will always be a mark of 'incomplete'."

Arielle says, "The same hall where Scott visited is called the Hall of Records—that's where the Akashic Records are kept. Most of us have all felt a desire to return to Earth at least once, and as you know, I have returned a total of 249 times. I either completed it, or had to go back and try again until I did...but I have one last desire that just won't go away."

Carole asks, "What is it Arielle?"

"To be a healer—and not just your normal healer, but one who makes a significant outcome to the future of Earth. I'd also like to return as a female and travel the globe, it is my last time of travel."

"I like that desire," says Grace. "What do the other two items on the board mean?"

"Good question, let's move on shall we?"

5
Blueprint Planning

Arielle looks at Elena. "Now, for the second item on the whiteboard. Elena, would you help me explain the process of planning a Blueprint and how some of it relates to my birth date? You are the expert after all."

Excited to be chosen for her abilities, she jumps up, and walks over to the white board, turns it over to the opposite side and then turns around to address to the group. "Well...let me explain numerology. Did you know it was developed by a man named Pythagoras? He was born in the same era as Confucius and was a mathematician and a genius in geometry. He believed that the universe could be explained by the properties of numbers and the relationships between them."

Sophia laughs. "I knew Pythagoras. He studied mathematics and astrology with the Egyptians and Babylonians—I think this is where he developed his 'right-angled triangle' theory, right?"

"Correct. And this lead to numerology—that every word and every name vibrates to a number and these numbers have specific energies and meanings that provide insight into human behaviours. He researched the numbers one through nine and found they stood for characteristics, abilities and events. Numerological energies also can be found in our birth names, but I'm not going to explain everything, rather only give you a short overview…so if you remember only one thing about numerology—it's the Life Path or Life Lesson number…just add up all numbers in a birth date so they equal one number."

Michael asks, "And what does this number mean?"

Elena smiles with glee as she finally has a captive audience eager to learn. "This number reminds or suggests an individual's life purpose…for example, if Arielle's birth date added up to a 'one', her Life Lesson would be something completely different from if it were a 'nine'. "

"Aren't there positive and negative energies associated with each number?" asks Sophia.

"Yes, as well as lessons and challenges she will need to overcome."

Arielle then asks Elena, "Is there a way I could work backwards? If I want to be a healer, is there a number that would support this occupation?"

"Yes there are, in fact a couple which, would give you healing characteristics."

David is intrigued. "I never knew this was possible…imagine if teenagers understood that the clue to their destiny, was in their birth date—this would certainly help in career guidance sessions…"

Elena nods her head.

"Yes David, if school counselors considered researching numerology, astrology, or any other areas of this field for clues, perhaps kids wouldn't be so hard on themselves. Children, adults and even the teachers would understand that everyone has lessons they must learn, or are suited to certain professions."

Jimmy hesitantly raises his hand. "Sorry to interrupt but where does astrology fit into this all?"

"Well astrology, both western and Chinese, are very similar to numerology in that they measure different energies surrounding the planets at the exact time we are born. Did you know that astrology dates back to the times of Socrates, Plato, and Aristotle? They all used astrology to help them understand what was happening in their lives and how to make decisions. Many leaders and royal families on Earth still see astrologists for guidance you know."

"It's cool that that this relates to mathematical calculations and positions of the planets," Benjamin says.

"Yes, but a natal chart is very detailed… so rather than go into it right now, I'll make sure it's ready for Arielle closer to the date she's leaving."

Arielle asks, "So, I can choose some of the energies I would like, then work backwards to determine a particular date of birth?"

"That's correct."

"This will help me analyze in what day, month and year I should be born. This is great!"

"So then there's only the task of choosing Arielle's parents. How's this done?" asks Carole.

Raphael says, "She picks them! That's providing everything goes to plan. Many planned conceptions never occur as the parents never 'meet up', or the biological timing isn't right—as well, the mother may choose to terminate her pregnancy."

Jimmy says to Arielle, "So if you had enough time, any one of us could be your parents.

"Now there's a scary thought!"

6
The Blueprint Timing

"That leaves us with timing, right Arielle?"

"Yes, Linda but there's no rush as to when I need to go."

Grace asks, "Raphael, how many years on Earth equals one day in Heaven?"

"One week in Heaven equals approximately 85 years on Earth."

"Eighty-five years?"

"Yes Grace, years."

Arielle continues, "Thanks Raphael, as for timing, I'm thinking sooner rather than later. My only problem is ensuring everything's planned perfectly. There is so much riding on this journey, soon I have my first meeting with the Council Elders presenting my birth date, lessons, suggested parents, my desire and theme. They in turn add their bits and when I know what is expected of me, I'll meet with my Spirit Guide, and together we work out the rest.

Carole says smiling, "I hope it's Cynthia for this one last time."

"Me too! She's great at handling all the research... attending lectures, finding information at the library, talking to other souls, Guides or Angels who can offer assistance to the life theme I choose. Then—the final step is to present my final Blueprint and if it's approved...I'm off!"

Sophia laughs. "I forgot how much work there is planning everything. I gather if anyone chooses to go with you, they must complete their own Blueprint?"

"Yes, but their Blueprint does not have to be as complicated as mine—they don't have an Archangel promotion on the line!"

Raphael jumps up says excitedly, "Okay, enough of how it's done, let's get to the brainstorming session! Here's the plan...I'd like each of you to think of a life scenario for Arielle—keeping in mind that healing is her desired theme. You'll need to tell us an overall theme, a location of where on Earth this will happen, and a synopsis of what this life would involve. So... who'd like to go first?"

7

Jessica

Jimmy remarks, "I'm ready, I'll go first."

Taking a sip from his wine glass he announces, "My suggestion…is for Arielle to be a female and live in a very strict religious environment…better yet, into a Mennonite Brethren community in Swift Current, Saskatchewan. Her name will be Jessica."

"Swift Current, where is that?" Linda asks.

"It's in the prairies in the Midwest of Canada," says Sophia.

Linda laughs. "Canada, eh?"

Jimmy continues, "Let's see…I want your life to be a little out of the box—I know! You'll have healing abilities…but not allowed to use them!"

Arielle smiles. "An interesting concept, go on."

"You'll also have psychic abilities, including clairvoyance, clairaudient and clairsentient of which will be very noticeable to everyone around...I think you'll have 'imaginary friends' when you're young—then a few years later you discover you also have the ability to heal by 'hands on' or pranic touch."

"Oh, like Jesus could?" Linda asks.

"Yes, that's right and although the Elders are impressed with your 'Jesus-like' abilities, they change their attitude when Jessica starts foretelling future events...which come true! At this point, your life changes forever."

"I can guess where this story is going Jimmy," Arielle interjects. "Everyone will believe I am possessed by the devil and try to exorcise my demons, right?"

"But prophecy is not a form of evil... it's mentioned throughout the Bible? In fact, every religion believes in the third eye, foretelling the future, messengers, angels and warning voices, so it's not an evil gift...but it does depend on how the gift is used," says Sophia.

"Yes, but the Elders are certain you are using your abilities for evil and subject you to some terrible demonic purging," says Jimmy. "After years of abuse, you pretend it worked just so they'll leave you alone. From that day forward you choose to keep your gift to yourself, virtually switching it off."

Elena jumps in. "But you can't just do that, she has the gift for a reason!"

"I understand Elena," says Jimmy, "but in Jessica's world it doesn't serve a purpose...rather it is more of a hindrance. Um...how about when you feel you can no longer bear the strict control of this environment, you run away?"

"Oh, what's next Jimmy?" questions Mary who's on the edge of her chair.

"When you're 16 and shopping in the city, you run away into the States."

"She's pretty young to be on her own," says Sophia.

Jimmy continues, "Yes and soon learns it's not as easy as she thought. On your second day on the streets you are nearly mugged and sexually assaulted."

Arielle is shocked. "Oh, poor Jessica...wait poor me!"

Jimmy continues, "It's part of the process Arielle. It is important for you, to learn from these experiences as it toughens you up so you have some street smarts... and don't worry, your Guardian Angels will be around to ensure you're not hurt. After eight months on the streets, you give up and decide to go back to your family—but they reject you and you're officially thrown out. At this point, you'll hitchhike east to Toronto and meet an elderly woman who takes you in for exchange for general housekeeping—one of us could return as this woman. In this positive environment, the real Jessica blossoms...you now have the freedom to develop your psychic abilities, you change your appearance and become more confident."

"Wait Jimmy—I am sorry to interrupt, "Mary raises her voice, "but there is a lot missing in this story! Why would Arielle select a religious environment and why particularly a Mennonite one?"

"Well...the Council wants a demonstration of Arielle's ability to deal with challenges, right? Well, being born with special gifts but forbidden to use them will make her life complicated."

"Perhaps it is not the Mennonite atmosphere that's important, but being part of an organized congregation or tribe," says Sophia.

"Tribe?" Carole queries.

"Tribe, community, colony, sects, congregation, they're all groups who share the same beliefs. Arielle could choose any religious environment...even an agnostic one," says Sophia.

"You're right, I'll not only have to prepare my Blueprint based on my desire, but I'll have to consider the environment where I live as well. I forgot how much research is necessary. Jimmy, your scenario is intriguing, what comes next?"

Jimmy shakes his head. "Just that you eventually become a medical intuitive...using your psychic abilities to see disease and illnesses in your clients. I haven't thought of anything else...it's just a brain-storming session, right?"

"I liked what you suggested Jimmy and it's a great start," says Arielle.

"Sophia, you raised a lot of topics for discussion, just out of interest, why is religion so diverse on Earth?" Michael asks.

"Well you've asked the right person! All of my reincarnated lives have had a religious theme…in fact my life's desire is to understand each particular religion by living within it's surroundings…" she laughs. "But I think I went a little overboard. You see I've lived as a Buddhist Monk, a Hindu, a Roman Catholic priest, a nun, an Altar Boy. I was a Protestant living in Ireland, a Jehovah's Witness, an Elder in the Church of Latter Day Saints, a Minister for Church of England and a Minister's wife for both Baptist denominations." She pauses to recall her past, counting on her fingers. "Oh yes, also a Muslim, Islam, Scientology, Judaism, and Pentecostal environment…so I guess you could say I am an expert!"

"A little overboard eh?" laughs Linda.

Sophia continues, "From my own experiences let me try to explain why religion is so important to so many humans. Most religious sects support a unified belief that there is a head of the universe or God. Many religions believe that the soul survives after death, although some have different interpretations of what actually happens when a person dies. Some believe in the Law of Karma—and that the future life of the soul is dependent only on actions performed during one's life. Others believe your actions on Earth determine whether you go to Heaven or Hell, or live in Purgatory. Some deem that there will be a day of reckoning...or Armageddon. Others dispute the subject of Jesus— whether he is the son of God—or only a prophet. Whether he'll come again—where others say he never came at all. It is important to understand that within the scriptures of The Bible, the Book of Enoch, the Dead Sea Scrolls or even The Koran, they are stories written about events that happened thousands of years ago, then handed down through centuries. The Bible for example, is a collection of writings by Jesus' disciples and the Ten Commandments were channeled by Moses—some items could have been misinterpreted, or could be open to scrutiny."

Jimmy speaks out, "Like Chinese Whispers...what is said is not always what is heard."

"Yes, exactly Jimmy," responds Sophia. "The underlying message is that most of humankind unconsciously worships their own God—but each person decides for themselves who this God is and each follows a particular form of faith which is best suited to his own essence."

Arielle says, "Both Sophia and Jimmy have given me a great deal to think about, and yes, the scenario of Jessica has great potential...thank you." Looking around the room, she asks, "Who wants to throw out the next idea?"

8
Feel Like Dancing?

As Arielle finishes her last sentence, Michael looks up and announces, "I'm ready…my scenario is based on a friend's former life—however, it's a little out there so you'll need an open mind, are you game Arielle?"

"Oh? Okay."

Michael starts with much hesitation, "Well…since you've asked us to be inventive…my suggestion is…"

"Don't worry, it's okay, no matter how bizarre," says Arielle.

Michael relaxes and says, "For Arielle is to be born as Lionel Arthur Johnson, a male desperate to be a female."

Arielle looks at Michael with a raised eyebrow. "Pardon?"

Everyone explodes in laughter.

"Lionel is a transsexual Arielle. An attractive male with extremely feminine features—you know…high cheek bones, slender arms and legs, a long slim neck and eye lashes, that most women would die for!" explains Michael.

"No need for us to die up here, we're already dead!" laughs Linda, "but I'll still take the eyelashes!"

"Laugh all you want, but Lionel desperately wants to be a female. He recently spent all of his money… on breast implants." Michael stops and takes a sip of wine. "I know this sounds far-fetched, but there are people on Earth who actually live these lives!"

Arielle laughs along with everyone. "Come on Michael, it's a little obscure…are you getting me back for one of our past lives? I said I was sorry."

"No, no! There's a story here…It's not all about you being a transsexual—you see Lionel had hoped to continue with the remainder of his operation, but he ran out of money. Instead of doing something illegal like prostitution or selling drugs, he, or rather you, become a famous drag queen."

"Costumes, make-up, platform heels…this is great Michael!" says Arielle sarcastically.

Raphael snickers.

Arielle says, "I'm trying, I'm trying."

Raphael smiles back. "You're being a great sport, I know I wouldn't be as calm as you are."

"I've never been a drag queen. I don't have to sing, do I?"

Raphael laughs. "Let's hope not! We've all heard you sing Arielle." Everyone bursts into laughter.

Michael is relieved. "I wasn't sure how you would react to being gay, but what about HIV positive?"

The group sighs sadly, "Oh?"

Mary interrupts, "But what about her healing desire? What about her journey?"

"I'm getting to that...being HIV doesn't mean Lionel's going to die. Come on guys, maybe by the time Arielle is born—they'll have a cure? I thought Lionel could help and work with those who have AIDS? I wish you could see the images that are running around in my head...wait! I have an idea," says Michael.

He throws his hands in the air and 'poof,' a projection screen appears. He snaps his fingers and the lights are dimmed. Then he points at the screen and says, "Voila."

An old-fashioned movie projector materializes with...1, 2, 3 appearing on the screen. Everyone claps at the new media format.

"Michael this is a great idea!" says Raphael, and then settles back in his chair to enjoy the short film.

Pictures suddenly appear and Michael says, "You can see from the images on the screen...our story is set in the interior of a jazz bar."

Mary interrupts, "Ooh, I love jazz! Couldn't we have a little background music?"

"Dark red walls, smoke thick enough to cut through, and of course a jazz band on a small stage." When he snaps his fingers the three-piece band starts playing music. "There you go Mary."

"Right on!" she yells. Her startled outburst surprises even herself, "Oh, excuse me, I don't know where that came from."

Michael goes on, "There are five people sitting in various locations throughout the club—four sitting in two booths near the back and a single woman sitting on a stool at the bar—when the camera zooms in, you can see an attractive Jamaican woman dressed in a leather skirt, royal blue silk blouse and black stilettos. Her perfectly manicured fingers hold a cigarette and her glass of white wine sits on the counter…this is Lionel dressed as a female and for the purpose of this presentation, I'll now refer to Lionel in her stage name—Leonie."

Scott, Saskia and Raphael look stunned at the close up shot of Leonie. Saskia says, "That's a man? Wow!"

"She's gorgeous, and let me tell you, I've seen many beautiful women in my days!" says Scott.

"No wonder Lionel is tormented—looking like he does. He could be a real woman and no one would know," Raphael adds.

Michael continues, "The band is in front of a red velvet curtain...the drummer sits at his drums, another hold his double bass and the keyboard player sits and practices a few keys. Then the drummer taps his drum which prompts Leonie to put out her cigarette, finish the contents of her wine glass and walk towards the stage, smiling. She's the singer in the band...they start playing...girls, you're going to love this one."

Linda's eyes brighten and she smiles from ear to ear. "Heh, that's Nina Simone! Fabulous!" She stands and starts singing, *My Baby don't care for show...My Baby don't care for clothes...My Baby just cares for me!*

Mary stands and too starts singing at the top of her lungs. *My Baby don't care...who knows it...My Baby just cares for me!* When the band finishes, they sit back down and smile.

Arielle asks, "I thought you said I didn't have to sing?"

Michael smiles. "I didn't say that...Raphael did! Don't worry, for the majority of this role you'll be lip-syncing...this scene was just to have some fun."

The music changes and so does the scene. "The next scene shows Leonie wearing a silver lamé mini-dress, microphone in hand...this time mouthing the words..."

Before Michael could finish his sentence, Linda recognizes the song and yells out, "It's Leo Sayer!"

She suddenly jumps back up and bounces around to the new beat.

"Come on guys, join me!" Linda encourages everyone, which they enthusiastically do. She snaps her fingers and a disco ball appears, then the lights dim and the colored lights transform the floor. From that moment on, and for the duration of the song, the room transforms into a disco. The guests bop their heads to the music and sing along. *You make me feel like dancing…gonna dance the night away…*

Arielle says, "I love it when they hold Studio 54 nights at Angels Disco, I must suggest a party before I leave."

Linda says, "What if you meet Leo Sayer on Earth Arielle…will you get an autograph? She continues to sings at the top of her voice, *I feel like dancing, dancing, dance the night away…ah a a a.*

When the song fades, the guests take their seats. Michael continues, "Leonie is a hit with everyone— in fact an entertainment agent from Australia extends her an invitation to the Sydney Gay and Lesbian Mardi Gras as one of their entertainers." The movie shows a scene of the Sydney Opera House, followed by Leonie on a float at the Mardi Gras.

The movie stops. The room is transformed back into the dining room. Michael carries on with his narration, "Leonie loves Sydney and the freedom to openly live as a female. Her health and quality of life improve, she permanently moves to Sydney and dedicates her life to working HIV infected people… several years later she writes her life story—which of course is made into a motion picture."

Arielle says, "This would be a challenge no doubt. I'd be faced with discrimination, then there's the matter of my sex change. Humans seem to have very little understanding for those who choose a 'different' lifestyle. God holds no judgment as to what sex you choose to dress as, or even who you choose to love, regardless of what religions may say, for goodness sake—we've all lived reincarnations as both male and females."

"But, this would certainly make your life interesting," says Sophia.

"It certainly would!"

Everyone laughs.

Arielle goes on, "I've been making a few notes, certainly, Michael's recommendation would have a different view on healing—what if I worked for the Bobby Goldsmith foundation and my healing involved palliative care for those with AIDS?

"I like the idea of your life being made into a movie Arielle, but do we get to pick the actor who'd play you?" laughs Raphael.

Linda shouts out, "I think Halle Berry or perhaps Eddie Murphy in drag?"

"No, Denzel Washington!" laughs Sophia.

"Nope, too big and masculine to pull off being a woman," comments Michael.

Everyone laughs and they all add their comments on who should play certain roles.

Arielle tries to regain order. "Thank you Michael for your enjoyable songs and entertaining movie, I'm having lots of fun!" Looking around the table, she asks, "Well, who's going to try and top that one?"

9
Medicine Man

Jason stands and walks to the front of the room. "Well...hopefully I can. My suggestion is for Arielle to be born in an indigenous environment."

"Interesting!" Elena says.

He continues, "I believe those born as indigenous humans have done so for a specific reason—perhaps their desire is to live on the land and protect nature? My scenario is to use my past life as an indigenous male living in the Haida coastal region."

"Hay...?" questions Arielle.

Scott suggests, "I think it is pronounced "Hi Dah"."

Arielle says, "Thanks. Sorry Jason, please go on."

Jason resumes, "The Haida region is located on the Queen Charlotte Islands on the west side of Canada. I've always had a fascination with native cultures—whether African tribes, Pigmies, Australian

Aboriginals, the Pacific Islanders or the First Nation Bands of Canada. Before the European's came, their livelihood was basic…they hunted when they were hungry, harvested plants and vegetables and protected their families or territory when necessary. It all seems very simple after hearing about the life of Lionel/Leonie…therefore my scenario is for Arielle to be born as Edmond Bob on a reservation."

Mary laughs. "Edmond doesn't sound very indigenous Jason…couldn't it be something like Little Cloud?"

"You can call him any name you want —the issue is his occupation…both his grandfather and father were shaman or medicine men, and I propose that Edmond is one too…however, he'll have a medical degree as well. I also thought of a twist…in his spare time he is working on a cure for cancer, and guess what, he's found it!"

"Oh Jason, I love it!" Arielle responds.

"Arielle, wouldn't it be wonderful if you found a cure for cancer? You could still heal through traditional and western practices, plus you can develop a cure, that sounds perfect!" adds Raphael.

Mary asks, "I wonder if all humans who reincarnate into an indigenous environment want to heal the Earth?"

Jason shrugs his shoulders. "Perhaps…only many develop alcoholism and diabetes you know…um, I haven't thought of anything else, only the plot. What do you think?"

Arielle says, "I really love this theme Jason, as this scenario could turn into a very rewarding life. I will definitely consider it. Thanks!" Looking around at her guests, "Okay, now who's next?"

10
Homeless

Everyone is talking loudly and laughing about the scenario presented. Arielle walks into the adjacent room and returns carrying a large basket filled with assorted chocolates.

"Chocolate!" exclaims Linda, "Bernard Callebaut!" she is delighted.

David looks inside the basket. "Oh great, Lindt!"

Mary smiles and says, "Oh yum, Haigh's!"

Like women at an end of a season clothing sale, all guests rush to the basket and madly thrust their hands inside trying to locate their favorite brand before it's gone.

"I thought this might raise our inspiration levels!" giggles Arielle.

"You know full well that we don't need food, wine or chocolates here Arielle," scolds Raphael.

She replies, "Heh, this is my party! If I want chocolate and wine…there'll be chocolate and wine, and lots of it! Besides, I have to must prepare myself for hangovers!"

"We can eat all the chocolate we want and not gain weight. I love Heaven!" chuckles Linda.

"Fine, suit yourself but I'm hiding the aspirin tomorrow morning. Now who's next?" asks Raphael.

Carole sits quietly at the corner of the long dining table. She has been writing ideas down on her portion of the tablecloth and, just as she finishes, she raises her head and looks straight at Raphael and says, "It's me."

Raphael is intrigued. "Carole, that's great. I've noticed you sitting quietly throughout the night. I know your last life was extremely traumatic…Didn't it involve several natural disasters?"

"Natural! There was nothing natural about them. I think God was using me as sport…I was an infant in Italy and I survived an earthquake that measured 8.4. Then as a teenager my family moved to Portugal where our tiny town was hit by a mudslide and destroyed our entire village."

Linda asks, "Oh…is this how you passed?"

"Oh no, thankfully my family and I were on holidays in London." Carole resumes her story, "In my early twenties I was in a train crash."

Linda interrupts, "Is that where?"

"No...not yet—I and another were the only survivors. It was a fire which finally got me. Our apartment building burnt down—with me in it. That will teach me not to smoke in bed!"

Elena acknowledges, "Not all lives are suppose to be that traumatic Carole, but I understand why you have chosen not to return."

Carole replies, "I suppose my past has influenced my suggestion for Arielle...I know if certain events are pre-planned, they will happen at some point, however what if Arielle were to return with absolutely no fear or apprehension?"

"What are you thinking?" asks Saskia.

"Well, for example, what if Arielle chose to live on the streets as a homeless person, living on food from garbage bins? Sleeping in a box or perhaps a young teenager who runs away from home, living in a drug house, sharing dirty needles and neglecting his or her body?'

Arielle joins in, "Perhaps they are simply lost and are searching for someone to rescue them, or something to scare them into fighting for their life."

"But they're experiencing ultimate freedom and independence from everything. They have no rules, no stress of careers or families or society's high expectations," Mary adds.

Raphael replies, "Don't think for a moment that they are not terrified for their lives—they have just given up…they're not living their Blueprint or even their life, rather just hiding…on the streets."

"I think I would be more suited to helping victims rather than living the life of one," says Arielle.

"That is certainly the easy way out—a healer in a comfy home is much safer than a healer on the streets…Raphael, does a person know they will have a difficult life from birth? Certainly God wouldn't let people choose a constant life of pain and misery?" asks Michael.

"Why not? If our souls are to fully evolve and if we have selected certain lessons to experience, each and every life we choose needs to be different. It wouldn't be very exciting living the same life over and over again.

"Ya, it would be like that movie *Groundhog Day*," interrupts David.

"Yes, that's right," laughs Raphael.

David adds, "Boy, I love that movie."

Raphael recalls, "One of my good friends, many lifetimes ago, once had a wonderful life—he was a successful banker, his wife was beautiful and adored him. His three handsome sons were intelligent and doing well scholastically. Then one day he came home and found his entire family murdered."

Linda and Mary shriek.

Raphael continues, "His grief was so consuming that he eventually lost his job, his home, and his life.

In one swoop, my friend lost everything that mattered to him. He chose to escape and live on the streets where society wouldn't bother him any longer. He begged on the corner for money, which he spent on alcohol, getting drunk to forget his pain. Twelve years passed and on one very cold winter's night, he passed away from hypothermia. Many people say that he ran away from life or perhaps committed a conscious slow suicide."

"I wouldn't say that, not knowing how you'll survive, fighting or begging for food…somewhere society must have let him down. Vagabonds are still humans with a soul, who once had a dream, a journey—they still do. They gave up because the world gave up on them. Surely they can be helped?" Sophia argues.

"Rather than living on the streets, could I suggest that I return as a Welfare or Social Worker? I could help someone like your friend get back on their journey, or help them somehow," Arielle asks.

Carole replies, "I guess my scenario needs to be a little more uplifting…what if as a vagabond, you… you have powers to heal! You're able to touch people and heal their wounds, just like that guy in the movie the *Green Mile*. What if you healed a police officer who was shot? Wouldn't that make things interesting?"

"Or to make it a little more exciting, two of us could return as your brother and sister who've run away and now live on the streets…you're searching for us—and the rest of us could play your cast as vagabonds," Scott says.

"Now there's a twist!" responds Arielle.

David laughs. "If I am coming back as a bag lady—can I request designer bags, perhaps Chanel?"

Carole says, "I guess this needs a little work, but is it a possibility?"

Everyone nods.

"Next!"

11
Guess Who?

*D*avid says, "I'm next. My scenario involves Arielle and her parents, who are young teenagers. Her mother is only fifteen when she becomes pregnant and gives Arielle up for adoption. Raphael, I need your help with the next bit…does Arielle select her adopted parents as well? If so, how is this done?"

"Excellent question, you're correct that Arielle selects two sets of parents. The young teenage parents would be written into her Blueprint, as well the adopted parents and you into theirs—and assuming she gives Arielle up, she'll have the second set of parents already pre-selected. Every child selects his or her parents regardless of the situation, whether they're foster parents, adopted, or even family members who take a child in after it becomes an orphan."

"But how would the parents find Arielle?"

"Intervention from our side that's how! Angels, God, the Council, Spirit Guides, …even spirits of deceased grandparents who push them together?" answers Raphael.

"Okay, now that we have that sorted, my scenario is for Arielle to be a Down's syndrome child. Her biological parents give her up for adoption, and her adopted parents raise her with all the love and support she'll need."

"You know David, some children who are born with Down's syndrome have no egos and have only one purpose…to love unconditionally. Those around them are extremely fortunate to experience such an intense affection," says Saskia.

"I've heard that, which is where my scenario continues…Arielle would heal her parents through love. You see, raising a disabled child is hard, and their marriage would most likely go through a lot of turmoil. The experience of a Down child is rarely for the child, rather the parents. So many couples feel they created an 'imperfect' child…and they have a hard time dealing with the stares, stress, workload, and reticule from others. If they knew their child was perfect—just with special abilities…and it's all part of their journey."

"Excuse me David," interrupts Arielle, "but I've already lived a similar life…it would have been about

15 lifetimes ago and although it was much different, could you suggest something else?"

David thinks. "Well, we haven't chosen the most obvious healing professions...doctor, nurse, veterinarian, psychiatrist, surgeon...do any of these interest you?"

Michael yells out, "I like the idea of Arielle being a psychiatrist!"

"Psychiatrist, yes..." says David. "I know...what about a psychiatrist who treats patients with obscure mental illnesses? One by one we could be your patients...causing you to look outside your academic surroundings—into something paranormal?"

"This is interesting. I like the fact that you'd be participating in my life...could I please encourage some challenging conditions...not just phobias of the dark?" smiles Arielle.

"Ah...you see, that's where you're wrong—phobias can be from this lifetime...or from a past one!"

Jimmy joins in, "Oh, that's a good idea David! What if Arielle brought through an unresolved phobia from a previous life?"

"Oh!" says Arielle.

David adds, "Yes, and Arielle had to visit a psychiatrist herself?"

Linda interrupts, "If she's clairaudient, she'll hear voices, right? What if her psychiatrist thought she was crazy instead of gifted...and locked her up?"

Arielle interjects, "Hm...I wonder if some schizophrenic patients are actually clairaudient... how would a psychiatrist know if I was normal?"

"I know—under hypnosis you speak from your subconscious mind. Or perhaps your therapist understands psychic abilities," says David.

"Interesting theory," replies Arielle. "Would the therapist accept this or think I was crazy? Hmm, this situation sounds intriguing! I think this could be developed into an interesting scenario. Is there anything else?"

"No, I was just throwing out some ideas...I could work on more, or should we move on to another person?"

Everyone smiles and says..."Next!"

12
Prodigy

Mary smiles. "I think it's time to lift the spirits of this party...I have a wonderful idea for a scenario...it will be based one my sister's past lives, but I'll add a little more pizzazz. Arielle will be born as a child prodigy—and have genius talents that will enlighten everyone."

Arielle joins in, "Do you mean a musical prodigy like Mozart?"

"Music...yes—I like music."

Sophia laughs. "I knew Mozart you know?

"You knew a lot of people Sophia," giggles Linda.

Mary carries on, "Did you know he wrote his music in such a frequency that it was found to have healing and therapeutic characteristics?"

"Music healing? Now there's a new one," says Arielle.

"That's right, there are studies on Earth about how music helps lower blood pressure and stress…in fact they play classical music in prisons and shopping malls where there is a tendency for aggression and violence," Saskia adds.

Arielle smiles. "Really, I bet the shoppers like that!"

"Not if they hate classical music!" chuckles Scott.

Mary continues, "There have been many gifted musical prodigies on Earth over the centuries so you could pick your musical category…"

David butts in, "Like singing…Charlotte Church in the UK?

"Yes and for piano…David Helfgott in Australia," says Raphael.

Mary adds, "And for Cello…Russian Alexandre Bouzlov!"

"But you don't have to be a child prodigy to be musically gifted," says Jason.

"That's right, but for those born as prodigies, their gift is more than a talent…their ability so pure and is brought forward from their subconscious minds—without the ego," says Mary.

Benjamin asks, "Do prodigy children carry forward talents from their last life? Mozart returned many times, and on each occasion, he was a musical prodigy, right?"

"Yes," says Mary.

Raphael chuckles. "But on his last return didn't he do something completely different...wasn't he was a plumber!"

"What about prodigies of academics, science or sports?" asks Arielle.

"I would think so," says Mary.

David asks, "Have you ever talked to a child prodigy?"

The others shake their heads.

"Well, I have many times. They are fascinating... they know their purpose...they retain their purity and innocence, and they never loose focus on why they're on Earth."

Linda interrupts, "I think I must have been a dance prodigy and have retained this knowledge even after I passed on." Standing she starts emulating a ballet dancer and jumps around the dining room. "I just get so inspired by music...especially disco!"

"Yes Linda, we all saw you at Angel's Disco, you dance very well. Didn't you make the DJ play your song three times? says David.

Linda continues dancing around the room, "What can I say—when I enjoy music as much as I do, it's only natural to want to dance."

She starts singing the words and dancing around, *Cause she was born, born, born, born to be alive.* She snaps her fingers, and the music is heard by everyone. Linda dances around until she reaches Arielle where she stops and pulls Arielle to her feet. Together they dance around the room while everyone claps and sings along.

Linda calls out, "I wasn't crowned Queen of Disco for nothing, watch this!" She changes her dance move to 'the bump' but gets a little carried away with a hip action sending Arielle flying across the room into Raphael's lap. Everyone bursts into laughter, then applauds. After laughing along with everyone, Linda and Arielle collect themselves, and return to their seats...exhausted.

"I think I'd better get to the gym, I'm already out of breath," replies Arielle. "Can't have the young girls showing me up on the dance floor!"

"Arielle, if you chose to be a child prodigy—what field do you think the world would benefit? Science, medical, mathematics, astronomy, physics, chemistry, music, literature, art—what else are we missing?" questions Raphael.

"What about computer geniuses?" Elena asks, "I heard that big software companies find young computer prodigies and pay for their entire education hoping they will invent the next big game."

Mary says to Arielle, "Well, I guess you can choose what ever field you want, but what an amazing life you could have."

"I enjoyed your idea, thanks Mary."

13
Silver Spoon

*L*inda stands up from her chair and walks toward the whiteboard. She takes the small blue marker and writes 'Silver Spoon'. Everyone looks at each other with puzzled expressions.

"What does this mean Linda?" asks Raphael.

Linda turns and addresses the group, "Well, my scenario is to provide Arielle with everything up front...then leave her alone and see how she goes."

Sophia questions, "Do you mean like royalty?"

"Hmm, I didn't think of that one, but no...I was thinking more along the lines of extreme wealth. However, unlike most wealthy parents who get caught up with the Jones' so to speak and don't care what their children do, Arielle's parents will coach her, support her, love her and encourage her to be or do whatever she wants. She'll have beauty, intelligence, creativity, other special talents and be the envy of everyone."

Arielle mocks, "Okay, what's the punch line, this is too good to be true. What's wrong with her?"

"There is nothing wrong, she is perfectly healthy, but let me describe her story...you're born into an affluent Spanish family; your father will be handsome, a well-spoken diplomat and your Mother, an ex Miss Universe winner who raises money for starving countries. You will be born not only with handsome genes, but also with great talent. From the age of four you'll master the piano, violin and cello far beyond that of your instructors. Scholastically, you'll receive straight 'A's and by the time you're thirteen you are fluent in five languages...oh and you enjoy painting watercolors in your spare time."

Arielle roars with laughter. "Linda, this all sounds great to me, where do I sign up?"

"I was thinking of a twist."

David chuckles. "Ah ha...there's always a twist."

Addressing Arielle, Linda continues, "When you grow older—you marry and have two perfect children. According to your husband and everyone around, you have it all, everything anyone would ever want, but are you really happy? This is your mission...having it all and making sure you are happy." Scanning the group Linda adds, "Lives of wealthy individuals are not necessarily perfect you know? It doesn't matter what you become Arielle, as you can make the best of any situation and learn and accept your lessons and the journey you have planned. The Council will be watching."

"But what about Arielle's theme of healing Linda?" asks Grace.

"Hmm, but with that much money Arielle could help heal by donating some of her fortune. Cash always will bring smiles especially toys for children, food for anyone hungry or medical supplies for anyone injured or sick."

Everyone raised their wine glass to Linda who in return breaks out in a huge smile.

"Thanks Linda. Who's up next?"

14
Tragedy!

Saskia says, "Let's see, we've had the touchy, feel-good story, so I think it's time to change the mood a little." She tops up her glass of Pinot and eats the last piece of Haigh's chocolate. "I'd like to introduce a new concept of collective souls and potentially Arielle's involvement in a group tragedy."

"Intriguing Saskia, why do you think Arielle would benefit from that particular experience?" asks Raphael.

"Well, I understand it is not appropriate for Arielle to be reincarnated into a collective soul group, however...what if we were? What if through our passing, Arielle's life is forever changed? Perhaps the consciousness of the planet would change because of it? We'll obtain approval from the Council for our deaths to be all on the same date..."

"Okay, thanks," says Raphael.

"Independently we would each select our birth dates, our parents, and create our own Blueprint's, just like Arielle."

"Are you suggesting an act of God like Carole experienced?" asks Michael.

"Perhaps a mud slide, Earthquake, or tornado, but collectively we pass as a group. Arielle would heal by counselling those who survived, or their families."

Raphael adds, "Many group tragedies have changed the destiny for several individuals and at times an entire country. Take for example September 11, 2001."

Arielle sighs, "Oh—what a tragic day that was."

"Thankfully those who have returned to Heaven understand that this was their journey. Some have chosen to reincarnate again as grandchildren, children of families or friends of the victims...others have moved on within Heaven," says Raphael.

Mary asks, "Do you think the victims knew they were going to die?"

"Well, no one knows when they're going to die exactly. Only God knows that. However, for those who lived, it wasn't their time."

David adds, "I bet they're actively working on their Blueprints now though."

"I feel so sad for the families who are still grieving their loved ones. I wonder how many Earth-bound souls haven't come to terms with their sudden and tragic death. Perhaps Arielle could be someone who helps the spirits find their way to Heaven?" says Carole.

Arielle says, "Don't worry, Raphael is watching out for them." Everyone turns and looks at Raphael. "Oh no, not our Raphael, but Archangel Raphael. It's his job is to work with victims and help heal trauma."

"What do the other Archangels do, Arielle?" asks Mary.

"Well, Archangel Michael protects the Earth when it's in danger."

"Like when terrorist acts become too extreme," says Linda.

Raphael adds, "The devastation of September 11 was suppose to be larger, right? In fact, the White House and other sites were potential targets."

"Yes, that is correct—perhaps Archangel Michael was successful in stopping further destruction," affirms Arielle. "As for the other two Archangels— Uriel, is the Angel of Repentance and counsels souls who have lived a sinful life, when they arrive in Heaven. Archangel Gabriel looks after pregnant mothers and babies.

Mary then says, "I have a question which is kind of off the subject, rather it relates to a past experience of my own. In 1917, my husband and I both lost our infant son only five days after he was born. We were devastated, not only about his loss, but that he was unable to start, let alone finish his journey."

"Who says your son didn't finish his journey?" asks Sophia.

Mary raises her eye brows. "What do you mean?"

"Perhaps his destiny was only to experience conception, or perhaps follow through with the birthing process as this may have been his first journey to Earth and all he wanted was a test."

Arielle adds, "Or perhaps his loss was actually planned for you and your husband? Maybe you both needed the experience of losing a child to grow into the next stage of your journey. He agreed to be written into your Blueprint as your child you know...even if it was only a short time."

"Mary, we know all about you adopting a little girl three years later," says Raphael.

"Well, yes we did."

"Wasn't your infant son reincarnated at some point in your life? As your grandchild?" questions Carole.

Mary laughs. "Yes he was and he was a little terror."

Sophia comments, "Life in a physical body is always a journey for the soul, regardless of the amount of time."

Arielle asks, "Okay. Who's next?"

15
Laughter Is the Best Medicine

"I have a different scenario…If healing is your theme and given as there are so many, I'd like to take your life to a more exhilarating level—that is healing through laughter," says Scott.

"Laughter?" asks Saskia.

"Yes…as a doctor who uses humor to help improve the day-to-day lives of sick children."

Arielle smiles. "This is great Scott, I love the idea that I can laugh daily. Children have the most beautiful and innocent souls; like prodigy children, some seriously ill children know their lives will be short. Their journey is to understand the process of pain and suffering as well as recovery and faith. I have heard some children say the most profound things and often wonder who's the parent, at times."

"Perhaps some of us could join you as the children or parents in the hospital," suggests Mary.

"I don't know if it is substantial enough for the Council to grant me my promotion, but I could use elements of this story. Thanks, says Arielle"

"Who's next?"

16
Medium Strength

"Right. It's time for some fun!" says Elena. "We've heard about Earth-bound souls as well as spirits and apparitions, so I thought we'd take a breather from brainstorming, to play a game."

"What are you up to Elena?" asks Arielle curiously.

Elena laughs. "Don't worry Arielle, this next scenario is going to be based around my own previous life…but before I get into it, I thought we could all use some entertainment. Let me set the stage."

Elena flings her hands up and the room becomes filled with candles, hundreds in fact. An organ begins to play in a solem and haunting way. Then the temperature in the room lowers allowing the guests to see their breath.

"Ooh, it's like a scary movie scene," giggles Linda.

Elena is excited. "Great, this is exactly what I wanted...the game is called, *Guess That Haunting!* You're all welcome to volunteer for certain parts in this game as the opportunity arises."

Elena flings her hands again and a mini screen appears. This time the movie is in black and white and everyone snuggles up to one another saying, "Oooh,"

Elena resumes, "Let me explain the game. I'll describe a scene—show you images and you must guess the movie...okay?" Everyone nods in excitement.

Elena announces, "First game!" Without saying a word the guests watch the black and white movie. It shows a television, which is switched on, sitting on its own in the middle of the room. The television station has gone off-air so the image is fuzzy. Sitting in front of the television is a small child. Elena asks the group, "Who'd like to play the child?"

David jumps in first, "Oh, I will!" His face appears on the small girl.

"David, your face is hilarious on that girl's body, you could have at least shaved!" giggles Mary.

The others share her amusement as Elena continues, "Great. Now we have David's face on a child's body, sitting in front of the television."

On the screen, David turns his innocent face, flips his long blond curls and looks directly at the camera to say, "They're here!"

Laughing, they all start talking at once.

"This is an oldie, but I remember this one," comments Sophia.

Carole says, "Too easy, it's *Poltergeist*, isn't it?"

"Okay, perhaps too simple. I'll make it a little more challenging. Try this one. The next movie excerpt shows a camera moving through a living room into an old kitchen. A young boy around ten or eleven years old is sitting eating his breakfast."

"I'll be the boy!" interrupts Michael.

Michael's face appears on the young boy. "Okay then, Michael is eating his breakfast when he says to the camera "I see dead people!""

Raphael says, "Come on, you said this was going to be harder! It's *The Sixth Sense* right?"

"Correct," says Elena.

"I have one more." The guests watch the next film, a camera pans out of kitchen window and into the upper window in the house next door. It then glides through the window of the bathroom and stops at a drawn shower curtain. The guests all jump and gasp when the curtain is suddenly opened. The movie does not show who is inside the shower, rather only a woman's scream is heard.

"Oh, is this *Psycho*?" asks Mary.

Elena does not say a word, rather lets the movie continue. The picture shows a headshot of a woman who looks like Whoopie Goldberg standing presumably naked in the shower. "What's Whoppie Goldberg doing in a *Psycho* scene?" Raphael asks.

Carole raises her hand pleading, "Oh please let me play Whoopie."

Elena agrees and Carole's head appears on Whoppie's body and Elena explains, "Okay, now Carole's standing in the shower."

The camera moves slowly down to Carole's shoulders and is just about to move lower when Carole yells, "Heh! Watch it. This is a PG rated game!" Carole then changes her voice to that of Whoopie Goldberg and says directly to the camera, "Oh, it's you! Yah, they called me back to work. Now that I can talk to ghosts, everyone wants to know me. I suppose you want me to channel someone too? Now turn around while I put on a robe."

Elena continues, "The camera quickly turns around as Carole slips a robe on and steps out of the shower. She wraps a towel around her head."

"Okay, you can turn around now. Follow me, as we're not doing this in the john!" says Carole in Whoopie's voice.

The camera follows Carole down the stairs to a work area where a pottery wheel sits. She pauses, then stares at it.

"Ah, it's not *Psycho*... it's *Ghost*—right?" shouts Jimmy.

Elena says, "Okay, perhaps these were a little too easy." The movie turns off and the dining room is returned it's original state.

Mary asks, "What about the *Phantom of the Opera*? I'd love to play the spirit of the Phantom."

"No way we're going to let you sing opera! I heard you in the choir, you can't hold a note," laughs Saskia.

Mary laughs at Saskia. "Don't be silly, I'm saving my good voice for when I next return."

"That was fun Elena, but you forgot about the best ghost movie ever made—*Ghostbusters*. I could play Dan Akroyd and search the planet for evil ghosts," says Jimmy.

Arielle says seriously, "Jimmy, you know that *Ghostbusters* is only a fictional story, that's not how ghosts are cleared."

"I know, but it would certainly be a lot more fun dashing around the city chasing giant marshmallows, than the actual way!"

"Okay enough of this game, let's get back to our brainstorming session," says Elena.

"Elena, are you suggesting I haunt you all...That would be different. I have always followed the light and returned. Are you suggesting this time I stay as an Earth-bound soul, or as a ghost?" asks Arielle.

Medium Strength

Elena shakes her head. "No this is not about you staying behind as a spirit, rather it is something more important. I suggest we're all involved and will then have different roles in her life. There will be roles for spirits, potential patrons or clients, a couple of Earth-bound ghosts who need rescuing, maybe a haunted house which needs clearing, or a spirit who needs a 'mood readjustment.'"

Everyone is talking at once, making personal choices. After a few minutes, Elena interrupts everyone, "Okay guys, let's continue. You know the Council will want to see a serious demonstration of Arielle's abilities so I propose she come back as a medium who channels entities and spirits by holding group sessions, helping people who are unable to come to terms with the passing of loved ones."

"I've seen a couple of shows on Earth about this topic…in fact there's a similar show on HeavTel, only up here it's reversed. The audience is filled with spirits who want to contact their loved ones back on Earth," says Linda.

Elena agrees, "That's the idea Linda! Let's watch the same show Linda did, but let me explain the program from my perspective, as a past psychic and medium."

She switches on a television then says, "This particular session is an actual show made in a studio gallery on Earth. Approximately 40 members of an audience sit in a semicircle. The audience is hoping to hear from a loved one who has passed on. The television scene changes and the medium arrives and stands on a raised platform. The audience watches the camera moving around them, then zooms in on the medium who is standing in the centre of the platform. In the background are the crew, moving around the room, carrying microphones and cords and the producer is hidden away, directing the show. Now...let me show you what the medium sees...the studio audience, their faces smiling all hoping to be picked. Now watch..."

The camera perspective changes to show brilliant colors not visable on television, as well reveals a fourth and fifth dimension. "Can you see the glowing entities in the room? They are trying to gain the mediums attention. Certain spirits are standing next to their family members, while some are standing on the stairs or sitting cross-legged on the floor. I'll increase the volume so you can you hear two particular spirits yelling out."

The television volume increases and the camera zooms in on a female spirit jumping up and down shouting, "Pickles, Pickles" at the top of her voice. A second entity, a male, is on the other side of the room. He is yelling "Prom night, pick me!"

The medium asks the second spirit, "What does Prom night mean?"

The male spirit laughs. "The back seat of my Cadillac!" The medium chuckles and mentally responds, "Sorry, can't go there, this is a family show—talk to me later."

The medium addresses the audience, "I am being drawn to the woman on the top row. I have a female coming through, someone who is talking about pickles?"

The camera focuses on a woman located on the top row with a red top.

The medium continues, "I'm seeing bread & butter, baby dills, and gherkin pickles." The medium points to the women in red, "I believe it's you, do you know something about pickles?"

"Yes, I love pickles. I'm addicted to them," says the woman.

The medium talks to the woman in the red top again, "It's a women and she is saying M, Mag, Margaret."

The woman looks startled and quickly replies, "That's my sister's name Margaret, Maggie for short. I use to steal my sister's pickles when she wasn't looking."

Margaret is showing the medium images of the two as younger girls, the woman in red who used to steal her pickles, and her sister pretending not to notice.

"Well she saw you! She wants to tell you she's fine and to get on with your life and to marry that handsome boyfriend of yours."

Elena pauses the show and addresses the group, "What you are watching is the medium's ability to talk to spirits, or us. The woman in red came hoping she might connect with her sister who tragically died in a car accident. The medium is now able to perform a reading for this woman and relay any information to this woman to bring closure."

Elena pauses. "Now watch this."

The camera zooms away from the medium and moves to the corner where two apparitions are jumping up and down trying to get the medium's attention.

Each is shouting out their own names hoping that the medium will approach them. "There are just too many here wanting to say hello, and it's only a 30-minute show."

"So, are you suggesting Arielle becomes a medium," says Jason. "Perhaps she could help with police investigations when loved ones are missing or presumed dead?"

He turns to Arielle. "Personally I'd like to see you help Earth-bound souls who are caught between Earth and our world, and bring them closure."

"Elena would Arielle have all paranormal or psychic abilities?" asks Michael.

"Well, that's up to Arielle."

"What are the different abilities a psychic can have Elena?" asks Mary.

"A clairvoyant sees events as images. A clairsentient receives strong feelings about events or people. Clairaudients hears spirits and claircognizant, knows things about people."

I think, regardless of the theme, I am going to have some of these abilities. The game was great fun. This is turning out to be a fabulous night," says Arielle.

17
Nothing...or Everything?

Raphael says, "Sophia, you've been quiet for a while."

Sophia replies, "I've been thinking about a scenario for Arielle...I'd like to see Arielle live a very long life— I mean a long...life!"

Arielle smiles. "What 90, 100?"

Sophia says, "Older! Did you know that there is a location in Asia where 40% of the population live to be over one hundred years of age? Imagine what you could do by living to an age over 100 or even to 130? They say the water, vegetation and atmosphere in this region are so clean and healthy that it promotes longevity."

Mary says, "Imagine your potential Arielle."

"I'd better have a good superannuation and pension plan then!"

"My scenario is for Arielle to be born in this same region and live to be well over a hundred years old," says Sophia.

Jason comments, "They call them Centenarians."

"Thanks Jason. Let me see...in a remote Japan village where she'll eat organic food, drink pure water and breath clean air. She'll have no fancy career with high stress levels. She'll have no musical or artistic talents, however she'll live a very long life being truly happy with nothing...yet having everything."

"If I lived in harmonic environment, perhaps I wouldn't need anything else. My challenge could be to just live day to day, happy, fed and safe, for a hundred plus years," adds Arielle.

Raphael asks, "Is that going to be enough for the Council Arielle? and what about your healing desire?"

"Well, I'd be living in Japan—so I could be the village acupuncturist..." she giggles, "for a very long time?"

"They call it meridian therapy," corrects Jason.

"Yah, that's better." says Raphael.

Sophia continues, "Healing can encompass so many occupations...think of all the wonderful people who dedicate their lives to helping others."

"Like who Sophia?" asks Arielle

"Well, Mother Theresa, for example."

"She's an Angel now," announces Arielle.

Sophia goes on, "Or doctors and nurses who care for ill patients."

"Healing is not necessarily an occupation but a way of life—a person who cares for the welfare of others...or comforts others by their gentle words." Arielle

Elena suggests, "What about a Massage, Kinesiologist or a Reiki therapist? That's healing."

"Yes and Tapping, Alexander Technique, Aromatherapy, Naturopathy," adds Mary.

Jason says, "Herbology, Hypnotherapy, Bowen Therapy, Chiropratic, Osteopathy and Physiotherapy."

"You know...a person can heal someone just by being around someone who needs their energy. Lots to think of guys—thanks Sophia," says Arielle.

18
Charity

"I'm next!" says Linda, "I know we have had some wonderful ideas, but as this is Arielle's final return to Earth—why not make it fun? My scenario is for her to be a famous celebrity...and in her private life she heals by working with charities and aid support agencies."

"Why the two sides, Linda?" asks Arielle.

Linda explains, "Well, I was watching a documentary on HeavTel, about celebrities on Earth who are helping world aid agencies...that Irish singer, and loads of American actors work with numerous foundations... celebrities have so much influence you know."

"And don't forget Oprah!" suggests Jimmy.

Linda agrees, "Yes...God has plans for her to become an Angel—perhaps that's why she named her agency after angels."

Raphael adds, "Wouldn't it be delightful to watch Arielle become a famous celebrity, and help those less fortunate."

"Certainly this is an example of humans healing humanity," says Grace.

"This is a simple theme Linda," says Arielle. "But I like the idea of sharing my good fortune with others who are not as lucky as I am...plus, I get a comfy lifestyle."

19
Time To Think

Arielle stands and announces, "It has been a long night…discussions, dancing, eating, drinking and laughing. Thank you all for so many great suggestions! Your creativity and imagination are astounding. But I think it's time we called it a night."

Everyone stands. They push in their chairs then swipe their arm across the table making everything in front of them vanish.

Before everyone leaves, Arielle says, "Once I'm ready, I'll need your help again to fill in some details, are you all willing to help me again?"

Everyone agrees. They move towards the front door, Raphael leading the way. He stops to open the door and both he and Arielle kiss each guest goodbye. As they exit through the door, one by one, they vanish.

Arielle closes the door and reaches for Raphael's hand. Together they walk back to the dining room and sit in separate armchairs near the fire. Arielle remarks, "There's so much to consider I'm glad I have sufficient time to coordinate everything. Right now I need a good nights rest so I can process everything. Good night my love." Arielle stands and leans over kissing him on the cheek.

20
Cynthia

Time has passed.

One day there is a knock at Arielle and Raphael's door. Arielle opens it and smiles when she sees her old friend Cynthia who says, "Well hi there!"

Arielle asks, "I hope your visit brings good news? Are you my Guide this final time?"

"Of course Arielle…and who else would they ask? Who knows you better than I?"

Arielle gives Cynthia a big hug. "That's fabulous news, come in, we have so much to discuss." Cynthia walks past Arielle and into the dining room carrying a large heavy bag of binders which she quickly dumps on the floor.

"I'm sorry I've taken so long to get in touch with you. I knew your last incarnation was going to be massive, so I've been at the library, and attending lectures preparing for today. We've got so much to plan." Cynthia reaches in to her bag and brings out a large three ring bulging binder divided into 20 sections—each identified by little tags and post-it notes.

"Cynthia, we've shared over 200 reincarnations, I just can't believe this is going to be my last time," says Arielle a little sad.

"You of all people must know how the turmoil my heart is feeling. How can I leave Raphael as we've never been apart for 249 incarnations. That's an awful lot. You know he's found me every time. Do you remember the time in Egypt when he was my nephew and he refused to leave me during a flood... we both ended up drowning."

"Yes, but he did try to save your life."

"Then there's the time my Viking mother abandoned me, it was Raphael as my Aunt, who took me in. When I was a Mayan Prince I searched all the villages for my bride. Raphael was a young maiden, we only needed to look into each others eyes...we knew."

"It's true, you've both shared amazing lives...his dedication and love for you are without question. But think what he is going through. He has to leave you on your own. He can only help from Heaven, but I am certain, he won't leave your side...ever! I've made it my mission to ensure you get this promotion

Arielle. Heaven needs another Archangel, especially with your qualities. You know I ran into Sophia not so long ago, she mentioned the dinner party...it sounded like you all had a great time. Did the group suggest a scenario that you might like to live?"

Arielle pauses, "They were very amusing, and a few were a little unusual. It's hard to know what the Council will deem as a substantial life...do they want me to heal the planet or just heal one special person?"

"Stop worrying Arielle!"

"You're right. I must remain positive. I don't want to stuff it up, and without Raphael, I'll be counting on you more than ever."

"I understand your concern, a lot is riding on this last incarnation, please don't worry, I won't leave your side. Oh, I guess that's right side to be exact." Laughing Cynthia moves to Arielle's right side. Then she squeezes her hand.

"What are you doing? Why did you move?"

"You should know by now...your right side is where your Spirit Guide is found, remember that and you'll always feel me. So, let's get started!"

Arielle squeezes Cynthia's hand and leans over to give her a big hug. "What would I do without you?"

"You'd be stuck in paradise that's where!"

"First item on the agenda is we need a date for your birth and a suggested time frame for when you plan to die."

"Doesn't God do that?"

"Yes, but we'll need to advise the Council how long you plan on living...then the Council will tell God. This date is written into your Blueprint...but once God says you're going, you've got to go back, and..." Cynthia says scolding, "I will not have any suicide attempts missy! Do I have your word?"

"Yes mam!" laughs Arielle. "Birth, I've chosen the years between 2003 and 2007—as for the month and day, Elena and I had made arrangements to meet today so we can ask for her help."

"Great. I'd like to hear how astrology will effect energies based on the years you selected."

"Out of interest, has the Council announced who will be your mentor?"

"You're never going to believe this...but the Council recommended three! Hippocrates, Ji Zhang, and Nostradamus!"

"What do you mean three? Why?"

"Since healing is your main theme, the Council has provided me with the best; Hippocrates for traditional medicine, Ji Zhang for Chinese medicine, and Nostradamus for clairvoyant healing and prophecy...together we'll be your musketeers!"

"One for all, and all for one!" laughs Arielle.

"That's right." Cynthia draws an imaginary sword towards Arielle. "We'll protect you always..." Just then the doorbell rings.

"Oh, that must be Elena."

Elena walks in singing *What a Wonderful World*. "Hi Cynthia, it's great to see you again. I gather you are Arielle's Spirit Guide again?" Elena kisses Cynthia's cheek then walks over to kiss Arielle.

Cynthia says, "Hi Elena, it's great to see you again. I'm so relieved you're here—I haven't practiced numerology for a long time, but I was ready to drag Pythagoras here if I needed him."

"No need to fret—I'm here and ready to help. Should I set up in the dining room?"

Elena places her bag of books onto the floor next to Cynthia's.

"I've done some preliminary charts already based around my conversations with Arielle. I think I've found a date where the energies are perfect."

Arielle asks, impatiently, "Well…what is it?"

Elena laughs. "November 25, 2007. You'll be a Sagittarian!"

Cynthia smiles and says, "Love Sagittarians!"

"You'll be a Nine and a Boar," says Elena.

"Is that all good? Should I be worried about being a Boar?" asks Arielle.

"Trust me, being born in the year of the Boar will suit you fine…Boars have marvelous personalities. And considering the importance of this particular life…you'll need all the help you can get."

"And a Nine, is that good?"

Cynthia jumps in, "Sorry gals, we haven't enough time to explain every number. The fact that Elena's reputation is on the line, I am confident that she selected the best possible birth date."

Elena nods. "Arielle, I had the best people helping me—so relax! Besides, I'd like to get your life underway so I can start watching your life...on HeavTel that is!" She laughs, "The producers are standing by ready to start airing...I've even got my fifteen boxes of popcorn ready..."

Arielle interrupts, "What? Aren't you joining me?"

I haven't decided yet, but I'll let you know soon."

⌒

Several hours have passed and the girls have discussed every possible theme available.

"I think this Blueprint is perfect. I'll present it to the Council and let you know how it goes," says Arielle.

Elena and Cynthia gather their books, then both quietly vanish.

21

The Council

The Council Chambers are located in a large sandstone building at top of the largest hill in Heaven. As Arielle approaches she feels like an ant next to the gigantic thirty-metre high front door. A large doorbell, shaped in the face of a cherub, is adjacent to the door. She pushes it...then waits. A few seconds pass when the door opens. Arielle is greeted by an enormous thirteen foot tall Angel with enormous wings.

"Hello Arielle, I'm Metatron. We're expecting you, please follow me."

Metatron is one of the largest head angels. He normally doesn't make an appearance at Blueprint Council sessions, so Arielle feels quite exhilarated to finally meet him in person.

He escorts Arielle into a large white room.

"Please be seated Arielle," directing Arielle to a single chair located in the centre of the room. When Arielle turns to thank him, he has already vanished. Directly in front of her is a drawn white taffeta curtain. After a few seconds, the curtain slowly opens and twenty-four elegant gold throne-like chairs are revealed. A second later, the Grand Council appear in their respective chairs. All twenty-four Elders, wearing white raiment gowns and crowns of gold, are smiling at Arielle.

"Hello," says Arielle.

Marmond, one of the Elders greets Arielle. "Thank you for coming Arielle. Have you prepared anything?"

"Yes Sir!"

Marmond laughs. "Sir...I might have lived more than a million years, but I'm not old! Just call me Marmond, okay?" Arielle nods. "Today's meeting is to discuss the formalities we require for your final Blueprint."

"Yes, I understand. Are you aware of a dinner party I had recently?" asks Arielle.

Another Council Elder named Zaspermus speaks slowly and with a very deep voice, "Yes. We were quite intrigued by your guests' imagination."

"I must admit, they did present some unusual ideas," chuckles Arielle.

"Due to the nature of your promotion we'll all have a part in the evaluation process. For example, I specifically will be evaluating how the specifications of your Blueprint match your completed life. How many of your friends you found—or who finds you, and how they impacted you," says Hamarkos, another Elder.

An Elder on the far right named Chimelu says, "And I will be evaluating the astrological and numerological implications of your birth date—therefore I need to know your birth time, what energies you will be born with and without, and what lessons you have chosen to master."

"I approve your parents and assess whether they match your requirements," adds Zaspermus.

An Elder Ubardah, says, "I discuss your theme with God and it's relevance to Heaven."

"How many days do I have to prepare this?" asks Arielle.

Ubardah replies, "As many as you need Arielle. The position will remain vacant until you complete your reincarnation. When you do, we will evaluate your entire life."

Arielle thanks the Elders, and seconds later they all disappear.

22
Love...
Is a Splendid Thing!

*T*he following morning Arielle awakes bright and
early. After her morning cup of coffee, she sets
up a workstation. At one end of the dining room
table she positions a computer, on the other end she
places charts of all sorts as well as numerous books
across the table. Adjacent to the table is a flip board
for possible scenarios.

She says to herself, "Right, I'd better get on with
this..." Like any woman on a mission, she sets off
with great enthusiasm. By midday, she has organized
several piles of documents, each relating to a different
topic. Two more white boards have moved into
the room and written on each white board are two
categories; female and male. Under each classification
there is a photograph depicting different lifestyles

and potential birth locations. Directly beneath each photo various charts reflect the life of the fictitious individual in the photo.

Raphael walks into the dining room. "Hi, how's it going? Need any help?"

Arielle, busy cross checking a computer program, looks up. "No, I'm going well. Thank goodness we're online now, it's making things so much easier."

"Oh, how?"

"Well, for instance, there's now a database of souls who wish to incarnate in certain roles. There's even a program that'll calculate outcomes based on my preferences. I'll be finished sooner than I thought."

"Well then, I best leave you be. If you need anything, a coffee, glass of water, just yell out, okay?"

Arielle smiles as he leaves.

She works throughout the day and into the night. Finally she turns off her computer, closes her notebook and cleans up the table placing her notes into an archive box.

Raphael pops his head round the corner. "How's it going? Need a coffee?"

"I need something!" she chuckles.

"How about I draw you a bath, light some candles and pour you a glass of port?"

Arielle walks wearily to Raphael, places her arms around his neck and kisses him gently. "I really wish you were coming with me."

He places his arms around her. "We've covered this already darling. You'll be back sooner than you can blink and then we can move into our new life." He whispers into Arielle's ear as he is holding her against him. "Tomorrow night, I'll organize a dinner for the two of us, I'd love to hear all about what you'll present to the Council. But for now, let's get you into that bath, and let you unwind."

A half hour passes when Raphael decides to check on Arielle. He finds her soaking in a cloud of bubbles—her head and feet have escaped the foam which has encapsulated her body. He sits on a chair and watches her peacefully resting. She opens her eyes to see him smiling at her and says, "I love you too."

He moves his chair next to tub so he can massage Arielle's neck. She relishes in the affection then says, "I'm so fortunate to have you Raph. I'm glad we're together to witness each others life."

He leans over and kisses her gently.

She pulls the plug from the bath then stands. He reaches for a towel and offers his arm as she steps out of the tub. As he wraps the towel around her wet body, he holds her in a loving embrace. And Areille says, "I don't want to leave you. You've rescued me from suicide. You've counseled me when I've messed up in bad relationships. You've encouraged me to try new experiences and you've introduced me to people who could impact my life on Earth. How can I live this last life on my own?"

"The Council have asked that you to do this on your own. Perhaps they know how much you rely on me for support and they've given you this task as a test. Although I'll not be there physically, I will be with you."

"What if I don't act on my intuitions or follow my destiny? What if I go off on some tangent thinking I have time later in my life? So many humans think they have…you know another day, week, or years to fulfill their dreams. Then one day they get sick, or have an accident and all those dreams are lost. This is my last attempt. I'm scared of failure, of letting my friends down…and of letting you down and not achieving this promotion."

Raphael reaches for a robe then helps her slip into it without saying a word. He places her hand in his, then leads her to the living room where a roaring fire is burning. He sits down on the leather sofa and invites her to sit beside him. As she snuggles up to him, he places his arm around her, providing comfort and affection. Then says, "I know the surroundings of Heaven feel safe. I, your friends, paradise…it is all here—why would anyone want to leave? Frankly, you don't have to. However you'll loose this once-in-a-lifetime opportunity. Do you know what a privilege being an Archangel would be? God selected you

Arielle, no one else! God needs you to fulfill this final story, on your own. All actions and karma of your last life must be balanced with any incidences that are in limbo...All wrongs must be made right. Once you close the chapter on Earth, you can help those as an Archangel. Don't forget, one week in Heaven is only 85 years on Earth, time will fly by for both of us."

"But what if I fail?"

"If you fail, you fail...No big deal. But imagine if you pulled it off Arielle? What new experiences would be presented for us? Don't worry so much, just go and have fun!"

She kisses him. "Well okay! I will," then snuggles back into his body.

23
To Be...
or What To Be?

*T*he following morning Arielle returns to the Council chambers and awaits the arrival the Elders. One by one they appear in their respective chairs facing Arielle.

"Arielle, are you ready to present your Blueprint?" asks Zaspermus.

Arielle walks to the lectern. "Yes, I am."

Taking a deep breath, she says directly to Chimelu, "Well, as you're interested in details...my date of birth—it will be November 25, 2007—that will make me a Sagittarian and a number Nine. I'll be born at exactly at 06:02am in a small Canadian community of Swift Current, Saskatchewan to parents who live in a Mennonite Brethren environment"

"And who have you selected as your parents Arielle?" asks Zaspermus

Arielle quickly answers, "Oh, that's right, you look after the approval of parents...well, thanks to computers, I discovered two old souls—Galen and Margarita, who left for their incarnation fifteen Earth years ago. Cynthia has talked to their Spirit Guides and learned that they are in fact living in a community like the one I require. I've also been informed that they plan to marry soon. As they meet most of my prerequisites, I ask for your approval on this choice."

"I will give you my decision when next we meet." Answers Zaspermus firmly.

"But they're perfect..."

I will advise you."

"Um, okay." Arielle is a little startled that he has not immediately agreed with her choice of parents. She reluctantly continues, "Okay. This community and religious environment are crucial for my Blueprint theme and lessons. I know it will be very trying."

"What have you selected as lessons or attributes?" asks Chimelu.

"Well...I'll leave the lessons up to you, but I'll need 'confidence'—so I can stand up to my parents and the Church Elders; strength to runaway and follow my dreams, and 'faith and understanding,' as I'll have intuitions and psychic abilities for a reason."

She directs her next statement to Ubardah, "My Blueprint theme is healing, then introduce a relatively new field to the world."

He nods.

"And for you Hamarkos, I'll blend several professions...a psychic, psychiatrist and medical intuitive then years later, a writer and lecturer. I'll travel and live in various countries so that I may experience different cultures, lifestyles and learn new techniques of healing. I'll meet as many interesting people as I can—some will be clients, others friends," Arielle giggles, "...and a few lovers and husbands thrown in."

He chuckles to himself.

"Arielle, I am curious about this blend of professions?" asks Ubardah.

"Of course...after becoming a psychiatrist, I will continue my studies in a new discipline called medical intuitive healing which uses my intuition to and diagnose diseases."

"How is this done Arielle?" asks Hamarkos.

"By reading a patients aura, or seeing their energy system – you see, people who have an illness have had something that has caused it...stress, traumatic experiences, bad memories, broken relationships— these all impact on a human's energy system and in turn their health. I'll concentrate on all elements of healing—physical, emotional and spiritual."

The Council nod.

She takes a computer report from her handbag and flips to a certain page. "My life will focus on four numerological pinnacles…the first is from birth to age sixteen."

Chimelu starts to take detailed notes making Arielle nervous.

She says, "During my development years, I discover I am able to predict the future, talk to spirits and know things about people without knowing why. Even though everyone believes these gifts are bestowed upon me by God, I endure dreadful treatment from my family and community. At 16, I runaway to New York which moves me into my second pinnacle. From the ages of 16 to 24, my 'dinner party' friends' become part of my life."

Hamarkos sits up, as this is his area. He starts writing down frantically.

"Their involvement is crucial for my Blueprint to be carried out—certain people encourage specific outcomes, others will introduce people who'll impact my future. One of my friends will encourage me to continue my education. Years later I move to Los Angeles…"

Hamarkos smiles and nods.

She stops and looks up at the Elders.

Some are smiling back while others are still making notes.

She goes on, "The third pinnacle is from the age of 20 to 40 when I move to Los Angeles. I continue with my education, graduate from university and intern in a local hospital. This is where I meet my friend, Lionel—who'll be a significant companion for the rest of my life."

"Oh, will Lionel be your husband?" asks Hamarkos.

Arielle chuckles. "No…you see Lionel…well, um… he likes men. He will, however, be an influential friend. In fact, we both move to Sydney Australia years later and there we befriend a researcher named Edmond…who is developing a cure for cancer."

The Council Elders are smiling and nodding.

"At this stage of my life, my intuition and physic abilities are intensifying. I am drawn to lectures and advanced courses as well, meet mediums, psychics and medical professionals who help me. My final pinnacle is from 40 years-of-age to the day I peacefully pass away."

"During my 40s and 50s I am well respected within my profession—becoming a leading expert in medical intuitive therapies. Later I'll write about my experiences—then travel the world giving lectures and seminars. In my 60s and 70s I revisit my favourite cities and countries and catch up with old friends, then in my 80s, I finally retire and settle down."

"And what of partners or children?" asks Hamarkos

"I'll have many husbands…that is unless you change your mind and let Raphael join me? Just imagine what I could do with my soul mate by my side. As for children, I hope for at least one child—a female musical prodigy."

Marmond says to the other Council members, "Perhaps we should allow Raphael to join her?"

"Absolutely not! This is a test for Arielle. God has made this choice and we must not give in to her whimpering," says Zaspermus.

"I wasn't whimpering...But..."

"If this wasn't such an important incarnation I would agree with you Zaspermus, but Arielle's promotion is pending her last life on Earth. Who are we to refuse her any assistance she might need for complete success?" argues Marmond.

Chimelu concurs, "He has a point Zaspermus, let's discuss it again with God. We can advise her of the decision. What do you think?"

Zaspermus says nothing.

After what seems like a minute of silence she continues by closing her notebook, then says, "I plan to live a very long life, and will die the day after my 111th birthday. I haven't yet completed all of my charts but I will shortly."

Marmond says, "You have everything planned extremely well, Arielle."

"Are you absolutely certain about all you have chosen?" Chimelu asks.

Arielle pauses. "Yes."

"I have reviewed the Akashic database to find four of your past lives left unbalanced. You must find that particular person, and make it right," says Ubardah.

"But what if that person doesn't want to return to Earth again?" asks Arielle.

"We'll influence their decision, and make it worth their while," answers Zaspermus

Marmond adds, "That is all for now Arielle. We'll be in touch with you soon. In the mean time, your Blueprint premise is provisionally accepted. You may start preparations for your final documents."

Arielle smiles and thanks the Council.

〜

Eager to finalize her details, she calls her friends to organize an impromptu luncheon the following day. Everyone, anxious to hear the news, accepts.

〜

Raphael prepares a wonderful candlelight dinner on their verandah as promised. "I take it by the luncheon planned tomorrow that you're ready to start finalizing your Blueprint?"

"Yes. I'm so excited, I think I have a wonderful plan organized. My outline was approved by the Council, however there was a disagreement between the Council on whether you should return."

"Oh!"

"They're going to ask God."

"Let's hope."

It also seems I have a few people I owe karmic resolution to. But once I finalize I'm confident everything will fall into place perfectly."

Raphael reaches for her hand. "When do you leave?"

"Oh, not for another Earth year—2007."

"That's good, I still have you with me for a little while longer."

24
The Cast!

The following afternoon at precisely 12:01, the front door chimes.

Raphael greets each of the guests. "Arielle's in the lounge room."

The guests briskly walk on through full of energy and excitement. The lounge room has been transformed. The table from the dining room has been moved against the wall, and in the centre of the room, is an enormous white sectional leather sofa—shaped in a large 'U.' Most of the guests are either sitting on the sofa or standing at the table fixing themselves a drink or snack. The guests include the original thirteen dinner party guests, Arielle's Spirit Guide—Cynthia, and her three Master Guides, Nostradamus, Ji Zhang and Hippocrates, as well as her two Guardian Angels, Albert-Charles and Doreen.

Arielle walks in carrying a basket of freshly baked bread and tries to find a spare spot on the table.

"Hello Arielle!" says Linda. "Let me help you."

Linda takes the basket of bread and finds a place for it. "You've out done yourself once again!"

Arielle sits on the sofa and motions for everyone to find a seat.

"My friends, I am pleased to announce my Blueprint has been approved. My incarnation will be on November 25, 2007 and I will return to Heaven on November 26 , 2118.

"That would make you...111 years old! What—didn't you want to live any longer?" laughs David.

"Very funny. I have combined many of the scenarios you presented at the previous dinner party, into one life. Auditions have now started and the casting couch is out there." Arielle points to a wicker couch on the verandah.

"If you wish to offer sexual favors in lieu of a role in my new life, I am up for bribery."

Sophia says out loud, "I haven't had sex since the 1800's, I think I forgot how."

"My darling, it's like riding a bike, you never forget!" laughs Linda

"Have you two finished? Can I now move on to why you're all here?"

"Sorry Arielle, I'll be quiet now," Linda pretends to zip her mouth shut.

Arielle says, "Right, while I explain my Blueprint, please feel free to help yourself to the food and wine. I'll start with Jimmy's scenario first as it involves my birthplace—similar to his story, I will be born a female in the Mennonite Brethren environment of Swift Current, Saskatchewan. I will have psychic abilities and, yes, be ostracized within the church. As you mentioned, my parents will treat me terribly and I will eventually runaway to New York. Now for the fun. I am looking to cast someone as the Elder in the church. Your assignment—should you wish to accept it…"

She stops to laugh. "I've always wanted to say that…will be to cause problems for me and do everything in your power to reject my psychic abilities and pronounce me evil. I thought of you Sophia, are you interested in coming back? Or would you prefer another role to play?"

"Oh, this sounds great, I know I could play this role perfectly. I accept, thanks," replies Sophia.

Raphael, wheels a whiteboard from the next room. He finds a marker and writes.

Mennonite Elder, male—Sophia

"Thanks Raphael," says Arielle. "Next chapter in my life…after I arrive in New York, I'll befriend a runaway teenager. Together we'll watch out for each other. This can be my Guardian Angel, or any one of you."

Doreen smiles and says, "I'd like this one please, Arielle. As your Guardian Angel, I think I'd be the best person to rescue you when it's the right time." Doreen looks at Albert-Charles, "Why don't you help too? Perhaps being someone from the soup kitchen?"

"Great idea, count me in," agrees Albert-Charles.

"Thanks guys! The next role is a Salvation Army representative...I see this person being older...like a grand father figure, very kind and someone who'll give me good sound advice. Anyone interested?"

Scott chuckles. "This could be interesting, I'd like to volunteer."

"Wonderful, Scott, thanks."

Raphael writes on the whiteboard:

Street Friend— Doreen
Soup Kitchen Person—Albert-Charles
Salvation Army Staff— Scott

"Then I move to Los Angeles. I need someone who will take me in and act as a mother figure, someone who encourages me to go to college and become a psychiatrist. This person will be someone educated, gentle, financially secure. She'll offer to pay for my education fees and might have her own psychic gifts."

Arielle looks to her guests. "Anyone?"

Elena is quick to reply, "I'd love this role Arielle, it'll be a blast!"

"Fabulous!" shouts Arielle.

Raphael writes Elena's name on the whiteboard.

Friend in LA—Elena

Arielle continues. "After a few years I complete my medical training then intern in a mental hospital. There I meet Lionel…anyone fancy being a tormented female in a male's body?"

"Um…Arielle I know this will be hard for me, but considering I lived the same lesson of patience six times, I think I need a change of perspective. Do you think I'd be suitable as Lionel?" says David.

Arielle walks over to him and touches his shoulder. "Absolutely! Just like in Michael's original scenario, we'll be best friends and we'll live in Australia!"

"Well okay then, I accept the role."

"Wonderful!" says Raphael and adds David's name to the whiteboard.

Lionel—David

"After I move to Australia, I meet a lot of people. One of those is Edmond—however rather than from the Queen Charlotte Islands, he is a physician working in an Aboriginal community up in the Northern Territory of Australia."

"Well, you know that's for me!" smiles Jason.

"I thought you might be interested. As for the scenario you suggested, you'll still develop a cure for cancer, in fact, I introduce you to a few of my medical connections so you can!"

Jason is delighted and replies, "Sounds great."

Raphael adds him to the board.

Edmond—Jason

Arielle looks a little embarrassed. "Um, this part gets a little awkward…I need a few husbands, any takers?"

Only men put their hands up. Mary protests, "Arielle, we might be female spirits in Heaven, but I can easily return as a male just as the boys could return as females. So what about the girls?"

"Good point, I'll take anyone at this point," laughs Arielle.

"I'll be one of your husbands!" says Mary.

"Me too," agrees Saskia.

"Ladies, this may be an experience we will laugh about for a very long time!" Arielle giggles.

Raphael adds Mary and Saskia to the whiteboard.

Husband #1—Mary

Husband #2—Saskia

"Next…I need someone who'll be either in medical research or a doctor, as this person will help Edmond with his cure for cancer. This person will also encourage me to become a medical intuitive and could also be a potential boyfriend, even a third husband…Michael, you interested?"

Michael says, "I think I might be in trouble, but I'm willing to play along, count me in Arielle."

Raphael adds Michael to the whiteboard.

Medical Colleague— Michael

"Jimmy, when I move to Sydney, I thought we could be neighbors, someone whom I go to for advice, coffee, chats about men troubles…you know the stuff," laughs Arielle.

Singing, he responds, *"Neighbour's, got to have good neighbour's*—ya, I'd love that. We can have some great parties, dinners and chats, I'm in!"

"That only leaves Linda and Carole."

"If you don't mind, I choose not to return. I'd like to participate from here," says Carole.

"I'm in, I'll go back as one of your girl friends, but can I be one of those leggy Australian beach babes?" laughs Linda.

Arielle is delighted and hugs Linda. "You can be whatever you wish…and thank you, I was hoping you'd join me too."

Raphael writes on the whiteboard.

Not returning—Carole

Girl friend—Linda

"But what about Raphael?" asks Carole.

Arielle smiles lovingly at Raphael and says, "Raphael's return is still being considered…the Council are talking to God. However, if his incarnation request is refused, he'll be a third Guardian Angel. Of course, Cynthia is my Spirit Guide, and with her team of Master Guides…I'll have many watching out for me."

Raphael writes the remaining friends on the whiteboard.

Guardian Angel—Raphael

Spirit Guide—Cynthia

Cynthia's Master Guides—Nostradamus, Ji Zhang and Hippocrates

Arielle reviews the whiteboard, and counts her guests, "Great! Everyone's accounted for, all that is, except my parents. I've given my preference, but I have to wait for the Council to confirm them."

Suddenly, the doorbell is heard and the sound of Angels chimes throughout the house. "Hmm…who's that?" asks Arielle as she walks to the front door. She checks by looking through the peephole and sees Zaspermus, Ubardah and Marmond standing at the door. Arielle opens the door in shock,

"Um Hello, is this a social call? Or is there a problem?"

"May we come in Arielle, we have an urgent matter to discuss with you," asks Zaspermus.

"Of course, go straight through," replies Arielle anxiously.

She shows them through to the library, which is adjacent to the dining room.

"After considering your desire, your outlined Blueprint and your previous past-life records, we wish to advise you that there has been a change of plans," says Marmond.

Arielle's raises her eyebrows. "Oh?"

Marmond continues. "Yes, a conception has occurred on Earth where the mother is due to give birth in two months. The soul who selected these parents has changed its mind and has backed out of his reincarnation at the last minute."

Zaspermus says, "We'd like you to take its place, and without Raphael."

"Yes, the parents, Sharron and Sean McCadie, live in Belfast, Ireland. They are devout Catholics which will give you a similar religious environment to Canada. Sharron is due to give birth between the ninth and twelfth of February of the current Earth year, 2005," adds Ubardah.

Meanwhile…Raphael is concerned that Arielle has not returned to the dining room. He goes looking for her and overhears Arielle in the library talking to Zaspermus.

"The parents already know you'll be a girl and have named you after their mothers, Caralyn and Ann. I am very sorry Arielle that you'll not have time to plan or analyze anything else, nor for you to personally cast your friends into new roles, however we request that you leave tonight!"

"Tonight? But…" Arielle says in shock.

Zaspermus continues, "The Council has unanimously agreed that your journey is to master this life, the life of Caralyn Ann McCadie. You must live your Blueprint through this child, with no further preparation from yourself!"

"No further preparation? But I'll fail." She pauses, "May I have a minute to think about this?"

"Certainly," says Zaspermus.

Raphael slips back to the dining room before Arielle walks in.

"Guys, we have a problem," she announces. Everyone turns around and stops talking.

"What's wrong Arielle?" asks Linda.

"Just when you think everything is going great, the plans change. That was three of the Council Elders at the door. They are waiting in the library right now. They have told me ..." Arielle stops and pauses trying to grasp the implications.

"What's happened?" asks Sophia.

Arielle takes a breath. "Well, a soul, which was due to join a mother, has backed out. The birth date matches my Life Lesson number and some of the Blueprint I wanted however, instead of being born in Canada to Mennonite parents, I'll be born in Ireland to Irish Catholic parents!"

"What's so bad about that?" asks Jimmy.

"Oh…they want me to go tonight! And be born in two months!" sobs Arielle

Linda shouts, "Two months!"

Arielle is now hyperventilating and Raphael helps her to a chair. After catching her breath she continues

"Yes, I'll be born somewhere around the ninth to twelfth of February 2005! They won't allow me to finalize my Blueprint details, take further time to cast any of you, or even research my background... oh dear!"

Arielle starts gasping for air. "I we've worked so hard on this Blueprint, now it'll be an absolute mess."

She's now frantic and places her head in her hands and sighs. "Oh this changes everything, I don't know if I want to go now. Raphael what should I do?"

Raphael, is his usual calm self. "Arielle settle down, don't be alarmed. If the Council feel this new Blueprint would benefit to you, who are you to turn them down? They must know something you don't. They are asking on behalf of God—and you can't say no to God! They know you want that promotion... they're not going to set you up to intentionally fail. Ireland isn't that bad, 2005 is a good year. I think you should go, don't worry, I'll continue the party and do the planning for you."

"You? You'd you do that for me?" asks Arielle.

"Of course, I'm your soul mate. We've lived together for thousands of Earth years, if I don't know you by now...I never will."

Arielle smiles at him and is comforted. He continues, "For the past few months you have shared your hopes and dreams regarding this incarnation.

Over dinner you described your Blueprint in exact detail. I'll try to match it as close as possible." He pauses then smiles back at her, "But I may throw in a few twists of my own."

"That's what I'm afraid of!" laughs Arielle.

Raphael places his hand on the small of Arielle's back and says, "Come on Arielle, you'll be okay, I won't let you down. Now go, before they change their mind." Arielle smiles lovingly at him and asks, "You'll still be one of my Guardian Angels, right?"

"You bet!" he nods. "Now go!"

Arielle says to her friends, "I'll see you all soon, promise you'll all be with me, okay?"

"We promise Arielle!"

Arielle returns back to the Elders in the Library. She says, "Raphael, Cynthia and my Guardian Angels wish to complete my Blueprint on my behalf, do you have any objections?"

Zaspermus smiles. "That's a brilliant plan Arielle. As your Guide, Cynthia can coach you—that is if you trust your instincts. But since you want to be a psychic, you'll most likely be able to talk to Cynthia normally so everything should go as planned."

Arielle nods and agrees to proceed. Within seconds Arielle, and all the Elders disappear.

25
Trust Me!

*T*he room is motionless. No one utters a word. Instead they sit stunned at the sudden departure of Arielle.

Elena is the first to speak, "Okay, don't panic! This won't stop our Arielle. We can still do this…what are her potential birth dates again?"

"Between the ninth and twelfth of February, 2005," replies Sophia.

"Well…that'll make her an Aquarian, not a Sagittarian and born in the year of the Rooster. Her Life Path number will differ depending on the actual day she's born."

Jimmy asks, "Elena, when will her soul join the foetus?"

"Well it'll either be immediately or she can wait in a holding space in the universe."

Raphael adds, "Cynthia, isn't it normal for souls to talk to their Spirit Guide while they're in limbo?"

"Yes that's right."

"Well then let's pick the date that would be most beneficial, and you can coach her?"

Cynthia agrees.

"If she wants to keep everything consistent, then she'll need to be born on February ninth," says Elena.

Cynthia stands up. "I can do that. We'll talk about this and I'll suggest a time based on her astrological chart...so count me in." She sits back down.

"Great, so we can make plans for February 9."

Elena asks, "What sex do you think she'll be?"

All reply, "Girl!"

Elena remembers. "That's right, she's already told us that. What do you think her name might be?"

David yells out over top of everyone, "Arielle said she'll be born in Ireland, so most likely it'll be Siobhan, Fiona, Sarah or something Irish like that. Care to wager a bet on the side as to what it will be?"

"I'm not waging any money with you, I'm still waiting for you to pay me the last bet we made over *Big Brother—Heaven!*" says Carole.

David takes out his wallet and removes $100. "Damian was the right choice to go...he should never have been there in the first place."

"Nice doing business with you, David." Carole laughs and pockets the money.

Elena goes on, "Well for the sake of this exercise, let's call our little Arielle, Fiona."

"Well I can do better than that—I heard the Elders mention Arielle's name will be Caralyn Ann McCadie, after her grandmothers," interrupts Raphael.

"Wonderful Raphael! A nice bit of eavesdropping!"

Raphael retorts, "It wasn't on purpose…I…"

"Calm down, I know, I was just teasing," laughs Elena

"Should we stick to the original cast or mess it up a bit?" asks David.

"You're terrible David! We have to stick to it. We promised to help Arielle, not destroy her chances. Geographically we'll have to change the locations though, rather than Canada, New York, Los Angeles and Australia, we'll use Belfast, London, Thailand and Australia," says Linda.

David agrees, "All right, be boring…but won't there be a problem with our ages now?"

"Why would that be a problem?" asks Scott.

"Well, quite a few of us were going to be older that her, in fact parent-like figures…If we count on 85 years for one week in Heaven…those who were going, now will be much younger," says Elena

Linda giggles. "And the problem with that is…?"

David chuckles too. "So…I'll still be Lionel, but a younger Lionel…living in London?"

Elena looks at the whiteboard and reviews the original cast.

"The role of the Elder was going to be Sophia, but it could be anyone in the Catholic Church, age is not important…a priest, nun, altar boy, or even someone from the congregation. Your main objective is to disclaim her psychic abilities and denounce Arielle as evil. Do you still want to return?"

"Of course—I'll go back as a Nun. Damn, I still don't get to have sex… I have to change my occupation one day!" laughs Sophia.

Elena crosses off what was previously written next to Sophia on the whiteboard, replacing it with Nun.

~~Mennonite Elder~~ Nun—Sophia.

"Great, we have a start. Arielle's next pinnacle was when she moved to New York. Cynthia, you'll have to work on Arielle to move to London instead, okay?"

"Noted." Cynthia writes it in her diary.

Elena goes on, "The runaway theme still applies… and with no money, and considering how expensive London is, she'll have to live on the street." Elena asks Doreen and Albert-Charles, "Are you both still willing to help Arielle as a soup kitchen helper and a one of her street friends?"

Albert-Charles says eagerly, "Of course, it is our job to look after Arielle and, considering everything's changed, she'll have to rely on Cynthia and us more than ever."

"Thanks! You'll be the glue to ensuring this theme stays on track for Arielle," responds Elena.

Doreen giggles. "I think I might change my character though…instead of a street kid, I'm going to come back as something more colourful…a surprise."

"Well, you appear as anything you want Doreen, just as long as you can help Arielle get back on her Blueprint path." Elena ticks Albert-Charles role, but changes Doreen's;

~~Soup kitchen helper~~—Albert-Charles
~~Street kid~~ To be advised—Doreen

Elena looks at the next category. "Hmm, we have the Salvation Army representative…we have a problem as this person is suppose to be a grandfather figure—Scott, will you still go? You could be younger, or have another role?"

"Like a police officer?" says Michael.

Linda yells out, "How about a fortune teller who reads tarot cards on the side street—he's suppose to give Arielle good advice, right…so who better than someone who can read for her?"

Elena laughs. "I like that idea…she won't mind if we change a few of the characters, right? So let's change the Salvation Army representative and replace it with a fortune teller?"

"Perhaps this person works along Portobello Road?" says Linda.

"Scott, are you interested in living as a female, wearing a babushka and large hooped earrings?" giggles Elena.

"Laugh all you want—absolutely, it would be a blast!" exclaims Scott.

Mary says, "Remember—you'll have to put the idea of becoming a doctor in her head…she must go to university!"

"Don't worry, I know what I need to do! I'll prefer playing this new role anyways, I don't have to be so pure," confirms Scott.

Elena yells out, "Well hurrah! This is going to work out just fine.

She changes Scott's role on the whiteboard.

Fortune Teller— Scott

"Now…what are we going to do with the next character—the friend in LA?" asks Jason. "Elena… this was going to be you."

"But I'm supposed to be a wealthy older female and help pay for her education fees…hmm, why couldn't I be a younger friend instead?"

"What if you're one of Scott's clients? You could be a wealthy celebrity, model or perhaps London socialite? Your age won't matter then. You befriend Arielle and could even become roommates. You can still help her out with a loan for her school fees," suggests Saskia.

"Perfect!" says Elena.

"I'd love to live an exciting role like that—we'll have a blast…going to celebrity parties, dinners, functions, we'll be the belles of the ball wherever we go."

"But don't forget your purpose, you are suppose to help Arielle. What you do for your own life is to be less significant," says Sophia.

"Don't worry, I'll make sure I stick to the plan," says Elena

London Socialite—Elena

"David, you still up for the role of Lionel?" asks Elena.

"Of course, though now I'll be a younger Lionel. We still migrate to Australia, but I think a stop in Singapore is due…I can audition for one of the Thai Boy productions, their female impersonator shows are suppose to be amazing. Perhaps I could be of Thai decent instead? In fact I'll look for parents in that region."

"When you arrive down under, everything will be pretty much on track—following Arielle's original Blueprint theme," says Linda.

Mary says, "Arielle's husbands and lovers can be younger…If Demi Moore and Madonna can do it, so can our Arielle!"

"We'll be toy-boys. Fabulous!" laughs Saskia.

Mary giggles saying, "Or toy-girls!"

"I gather you're both still in?" asks Elena.

They both agree, "Absolutely, we wouldn't miss this, not now!"

"That leaves Jimmy and Michael. Are you still interested in being the medical colleague and Jimmy, the neighbour?" asks Elena.

"Of course, this little game is turning out to be the incarnation of the century. I'm not going to miss out, count me in."

"Arielle will be so upset that she wasn't the youngest in our group. I know I'll have fun rubbing that in for at least a thousand years," chuckles Jimmy.

"Carole, are you still planning to stay here?"

Carole breaks out in laughter. "No way! This is going to be hilarious and I think the one life I'll enjoy trying. Just think how we'll all laugh when we return…I'll be Arielle's daughter…the prodigy child that Arielle wants, but I'll be a rebellious child. I'll advise the Council of my selection for Arielle as my mother—I guess that will leave either Saskia or Mary as my father."

Elena doubles up. "Oh no, poor Arielle."

Saskia and Mary say together, "No poor us!" They point to each other saying, "I hope she picks you!"

Elena summaries. "Well, we have a full complement. Let me confirm the final roles." She places a tick beside each name.

Lionel—David.
Edmond—Jason

Husband #1—Mary
Husband #2—Saskia

For Carole, she writes…

Arielle's prodigy daughter—Carole

She pauses over Linda's name. Linda smiles, "I'm still in."

Girlfriend—Linda.

Raphael says to the whole group, "Since everyone is returning, I think you'd better start working on your own Blueprints…the Council Elders will most likely give you urgent approval so you won't miss out."

Elena and Jimmy confer. Elena then says, "Jimmy and I are going to work on ours together, so if you don't mind, we're going to leave now." Elena and Jimmy kiss the other guest's good-bye, and then vanish. The other guests all walk to the front door, kiss Arielle and Raphael goodbye, and as they leave, they too vanish.

26
It's Time

Doreen and Albert-Charles arrive at Raphael's home to announce with great excitement, "I just got an SMS from Archangel Gabriel...Arielle's about to be born." Says Doreen.

Albert-Charles says, "Let's go and watch from the delivery room."

～

Raphael, Albert-Charles and Doreen greet Cynthia and the Master Guides who are already sitting in the observation deck above the delivery table.

"Push...one more time Sharron," says the doctor. With one last big push, Arielle new body is released into the gravity of Earth. "She's not breathing," states the nurse, "come on little one!"

"Come on...breathe!" says Doreen.

A few seconds pass...the little girl gasps for air then starts to cry.

Applause breaks out from the group in the observation room.

"Hurrah! Our little Arielle is born!" says Cynthia

"Time of birth 06:02 February 9, 2005," says the doctor to the nurse, "please write that down for the birth certificate."

"Great work Cynthia, you got the time and date perfect!   Guess I owe you a bottle of champagne now!" congratulates Raphael.

"And is her name the same?" asks Doreen

"Caralyn Ann McCadie." Says Cynthia proudly.

"Boy is she in for one hell of a life!" laughs Albert-Charles.

Raphael chuckles. "Yes she is, and I can't wait to watch."

27

The Year 2116

Arielle is lying in a hospital bed, tubes are inserted throughout her fragile body. Her heart is monitored by a machine and she is breathing into an oxygen cup, but at 111 years old, she's happy.

She opens her eyes. She removes the breathing apparatus and talks out loud, "Well Hello!"

The nurse in the room asks, "Who are you talking to Miss?"

Arielle does not answer instead continues talking out loud, "It's so good to see you…" Her lungs are weak, so she takes a breath from the apparatus, then continues, "I've been waiting for you all to arrive…" pausing again to catch her breath, "it's time isn't it?" Arielle smiles and continues speaking to spirits who are now filling the room, "I've been waiting for this moment for over one hundred years…Boy, what a life!"

One of her friends steps out from the crowd. "Hello Arielle, we're all here."

One-by-one the spirits of her dinner party friends appear. Other spirits from Heaven have also come to join in the celebration—and fill the room. In the crowd she recognizes her mother and says, "Mother, you were fabulous! An Oscar goes to you…"

She recognizes Elena. "What a fabulous friend you were!" Then notices her friend Carole. "I'm sorry. I'll explain later."

Arielle looks around the room. "Raphael…where's my beloved Raphael?"

Raphael walks out from the back of the crowd to see his beautiful partner smiling lovingly. Tears well up in both their eyes, he leans over and gives her a loving, soft kiss on her lips. Arielle reaches up with her frail hands and touches his face saying, "I may have had a few too many husbands this life…but none matched the love I feel for you!"

Raphael beams.

Arielle looks around the room smiling at her friends.

"You don't need to hang on any more Arielle, just let yourself go." Says one of the friends.

Arielle smiles. Her complexion becomes transparent…the heart monitor triggers an alarm which sends the doctors and nurses running into the room. Arielle closes her eyes and says, "Thank you all for being here with me, and bringing me home."

She suddenly opens her eyes, turns and looks straight at the doctor and says, "Thank you for your efforts, but I'm ready to go now."

Her eyes close.

The heart monitor sounds a flat line...minutes later—the equipment is turned off.

The doctor turns and smiles to the nurses. "Time of death, 23:11 on February 10, 2116...My what a lady!"

At the moment of her death, Arielle's soul detaches itself from her physical body and ascend towards the ceiling. The room, building and hospital disappear while her body floats up along side her friends. Many fly over to touch, hug and escort her to the white light. Now feeling young and lively, with no tubes, ailments, or frailty...she floats over to Raphael, throws her arms around his neck and holds on tight. He whispers, "Welcome home my love! I'm glad you're back."

THE END

An overview of Mennonite Brethren

This information has come from many sources, and has taken considerable research to collect some of the early history of our family. I have studied history books, encyclopedias, and the writings of C. Henry Smith and Charles S Braden. Some general information has come from a German novel called the 'The Snow King' (title translated). I have some information from older people about my family and events of which they have personal knowledge. Several people who have lived in Sweden have given me a further insight into the past. Some information has come from the records left by my grandfather and my parents who told me of their experiences, and things that were passed on to them by their elders.

Because of conditions in Europe, it was necessary for marriages to be restricted to only those of their own faith. As a result, the Mennonites intermarried until they are now considered an ethnic group as well as a denomination.

A short summary of some of the religious events which took place in Europe may help you to understand better.

Anabaptists

Means again to baptize, or those who believe in a second baptism because 1) their first baptism took place in infancy or because 2) their first baptism is invalid for some reason.

The question of proper baptism arose early in the third century when a severe controversy developed between Eastern and Western churches over the validity of baptism. St Augustine, Bishop of Carthage, the Eastern churches maintained that under certain circumstances, baptism must be repeated to be considered valid.

In 253, Stephen-Bishop of Rome, excommunicated the Bishops of Asia Minor derisively calling them Anabaptists.

In the 16th Century Europe, the Anabaptists arose as an extreme revolutionary sect of the reformation. Although repudiated by Luther and his followers, the sect had its' origin in the teaching of a Lutheran pastor, Thomas Munzer, from Zwickau, Saxony. He began preaching in 1521 the doctrine of adult baptism, and complete freedom from Civil and religious authority. He incited the peasants of South and Middle Germany to revolt against their Lords, thereby bringing about the Peasants War in which the peasants were defeated and Munzer and other leaders were executed (1525).

With the death of Munzer, new leaders arose, among them John Bochold of Leyden and Knipperdolling,

Counsellor of Munster. The inhabitants of Munster enthusiastically adopted the radical teachings of a new sect and Bochold, adopting the title of John of Leyden, announced himself as king of New Zion, (the name Anabaptists gave to their kingdom). Munster then became a town in which all manner of excesses of fanaticism, lust and cruelty were practiced. Bochold lived in luxury and ruled with an iron hand, executing any who held differing views, or opposed him. In 1535, several Protestant princes united with the Bishop and took the city, following which they tortured to death the leaders of the Anabaptists.

Meanwhile, the movement had spread to Amsterdam, where the Anabaptists repudiated the principals of community of goods and women as practiced by the Munster radicals and instead advocated a new kingdom of pure Christians. Their leader, David Joris, a mystic theologian attracted many adherents. However, because of persecution, he was forced to withdraw, and want to Basel, where he joined the communion of the Reformed Church.

The fanatical period of the Anabaptists ended with the episode at Munster. Later Menno Simmons organized a conservative Anabaptists of the Netherlands and Germany, who repudiated the fanatical doctrines of the Munster radicals. The Mennonites (deriving their name from Menno Simmons) disavow infant baptism, but have nothing in common with the radical beliefs and practices of the Munster Anabaptists of the 16th Century.

Mennonites began as a denomination of evangelical Christian Protestants in a congregation formed in Zurich in 1525 by Conrad Grebel, Manz and Blaurok and others.

The group in Zurich separated itself from the State Church because they believed that the bible did not sanction civil authority. Although they believed in obeying the government of State, they upheld the principles of refusing to bear arms, to participate in civil duties and to take oaths. The two sacraments they retained were baptism of adults and the Lord's Supper. The Bible was accepted as their only guide of faith. The Mennonite Confession of Faith was adopted in Dort, Poland in 1632.

Persecution came to all who opposed the Catholic or State Church. As result the Mennonites were scattered all over Northern Europe. The refusal to bear arms was especially hard on the Mennonites who had settled in warlike Germany.

The offer of land and freedom from military service came from Catherine II of Russia (1762-1796) seemed like a Godsend to these beleaguered people. Most of them flocked into Russia at this time. They stayed until the take over of Communism made many leave the country. However some of them stayed in Russia. Many of them lost their lives, some of them were integrated with the Communist Russian society.

My family were among those who left Russia. Today we find Mennonite communities in North and South America, and Mexico.

Norman Nickel
(my Mother's cousin and now in Heaven)

So what happened to Arielle?
Does she get her promotion?

Book Two of Three—to be released 2007
GAMES OF FATE

Arielle's incarnation is now in action...on February 9, 2005, Arielle is incarnated and born as Caralyn Ann McCadie. Sharron and Sean McCadie are strict Irish Catholic parents and when Arielle starts showing mysterious behaviours of foreseeing the future, reading minds as well as hearing and seeing spirits—the McCadie's believe their daughter is possessed.

For fifteen years, Caralyn is subjected to tests, exorcisms, baptisms and even several months in a mental hospital. On her sixteenth birthday, Caralyn runs away to London. Penniless and scared, she takes shelter in a cardboard box, however, days later Caralyn is robbed of what little money she has managed to earn and forced to steal food to survive. A colourful prostitute named Doreen, appears out of no where and rescues Caralyn from a life on the streets and finds her employment in a café.

But is this Caralyn's 'destiny'? Covering a period of over one hundred years, the original 'Blueprint' dinner guests appear in Caralyn's life fulfilling various supportive roles; friends, lovers, neighbour's, classmates, employers, strangers, and spirits from Heaven are all involved to ensure Caralyn's (or rather Arielle's) Blueprint is completed.

Book Three of Three—to be released 2007/08
ARCH OF THE ANGEL

*A*rielle must now meet with the Council and justify her final incarnation. But before this happens, she must have her life evaluated by the recorder of the Akashic Records. All karmic debts, lessons, and details of her Blueprint are examined.

While she waits for ther Council's decision, Arielle plans a dinner party. All of the friends who participated in Blueprint and Games of Fate tell their stories of how they were involved in Arielle's life.

Order Form

Title	Cost	Number Ordered	Total
Blueprint	$27.95 AUD		
Games of Fate	$27.95 AUD		
Arch of the Angel	$27.95 AUD		
P&H one to three books	$5		
P&H four or more books	$7.50		
TOTAL			

Name: ....

Address: ....

....

Postcode/Zip:........................State/Province:..............................

Country:...

I/we enclose a cheque/money order/ credit card authorisation

Total amount enclosed/authorised $AUD..

Please debit my VISA ☐ MasterCard ☐

☐☐☐☐ ☐☐☐☐ ☐☐☐☐ ☐☐☐☐

Name on card:...

Signature:..

Expiry Date:...

Send To:
Ruby Read Publishing
PO Box R724
Royal Exchange Postal Centre
Sydney NSW Australia 1225